"We meet again

Holly whirled around and looked up into the gray eyes of the *mann* she'd met the day before. "Oh, hello."

"*Gutentag.* You wish to buy something?"

Holly shook her head. "Not really. I was just wandering a little."

The *mann* looked at her with curiosity. "I think you do not tell the whole truth. You seemed to be looking for something in particular."

Holly was amazed and huffed out a short laugh. "You would be right. Are you a mind reader?"

He smiled. "*Nee*, just observant." He looked over her shoulder for a moment and then returned his attention to her. "My name is Evan Miller."

Holly extended her hand, and then let it drop when he merely looked at it. Strange and a bit rude, she thought. Maybe because she was a stranger and a woman? In her world she would have been offended, but she wasn't in her world, and differences of cultural practice had to be accepted. She rubbed her palm on her thigh and then smiled. "I'm Holly Sanders."

Hannah Schrock is the bestselling author of numerous Amish romance and Amish mystery books.

THE AMISH ORPHAN

Hannah Schrock

ISBN-13: 978-1-335-49977-6

The Amish Orphan

First published in 2016 by Burton Crown Ltd.
This edition published in 2020.

Recycling programs
for this product may
not exist in your area.

This edition published by arrangement with Harlequin Books S.A.

For questions and comments about the quality of this book,
please contact us at CustomerService@Harlequin.com.

Harlequin Enterprises ULC
22 Adelaide St. West, 40th Floor
Toronto, Ontario M5H 4E3, Canada
www.Harlequin.com

Printed in U.S.A.

THE AMISH ORPHAN

Prologue

Evan Miller awoke from his slumber believing he had been dreaming about meat being cooked on a grill. Indeed, his mouth was almost salivating at the thought. Maybe he had drifted off after a hard day in the fields and someone somewhere had decided to eat outside.

But then he heard the cries and the unmistakeable sound of panic. The realisation hit him that the smoke that had awoken him wasn't the soft sweet smell of the grill but of the thick, acrid sort that signified something far more sinister.

A heavy banging on the door brought him to his senses.

"Evan, get up! Quick. There's a fire." He couldn't identify the voice, but that was irrelevant at the moment.

A barn was inevitably alight somewhere.

The men of the community would pass buckets from one another in an attempt to extinguish the flames. He had been part of such endeavours in the past but rarely had the fires been brought under control. No doubt there would be a barn raising in the spring. But there would be someone's livelihood at risk, so they all had to do what they could to help at this moment.

He leapt out of bed and pulled on his shirt and pants. He realised that he could see perfectly despite it being the dead of night. A deep orange glow was flickering from the window. He rubbed his eyes to erase the last remnants of sleep and the view outside started to make sense. The full horror hit him like a horse's kick in the stomach.

This was no barn fire.

A haus was ablaze.

The flames licked the sky as they danced across the rooftop and down the white walls to the porch hungrily consuming all in their path.

It was a house that he knew well. Too well.

It was Naomi and Harley's place.

His sister and brother-in-law.

And his niece. His beautiful little fun loving niece, Becca.

He turned and ran for the door.

Evan sprinted across his garden and leapt over the short white fence into the fields. He charged towards the flames, feeling the heat intensify with every step he took. By the time he reached the house, his lungs were gasping for air, but this only meant he coughed as the thickness of the foul tasting smoke clogged his passageways.

He paused for a second taking in the situation, but his brain couldn't process what he was seeing, it was too much.

How could the flames leap so high, he thought stupidly as he watched them stretch towards the heavens.

"They're still inside," he heard someone shout.

"No," Evan screamed and started running towards the haus.

Evan was stopped dead in his tracks by the strong right arm of Noah Schwartz.

"Stop you fool," Noah cried. "The flames are too much. You'll never get inside."

Evan shook his head, refusing to accept what was obvious to everyone else. "But I got to try," he insisted and pushed Noah aside and ran as close as he could to the front door of his sister's burning house. He instinctively raised his arm in front of his face to protect it from the heat. He took two steps further forward, but could not go further.

"Naomi!" he screamed at the top of his voice.

But only the cracking and hiss of the flames answered him back as though they were mocking him. In a spine-chilling instant, he realized in horror that Noah had been right. The fire and the heat were just too intense.

A wall of flame faced him. Getting inside was impossible.

Then, out of the smoke, he saw a tall Amish man carrying a child in his arms. It was John King, a mountain of a man, fabled for pulling his plough over his field himself when his horse had taken lame.

"Becca," Evan cried in relief, running over towards his niece, but she just looked up at him blankly as though she couldn't even see that he was there.

"My schweschder?" Evan pressed John. "Harley?"

John shook his head as he looked at Evan with eyes full of horrors that he wished he had never seen.

Suddenly there was a noise like thunder as the roof, weakened by the fire collapsed.

All hope was gone.

Gott spoke silently to him, and he knew in a moment what he had to do. He bent down over the still form of the little girl and took her hand. "Don't worry, Becca," he whispered. "I'll look after you."

And then he slumped to his knees and let the tears fall down his face.

Part One

Christmas

Born and Raised

Philadelphia, Pennsylvania, a few weeks before Christmas...

Holly Sanders turned her head as the voices of excited people drifted from the direction of the escalator. It was the week after Thanksgiving and the newspaper office where she worked was decorated for the Christmas Season. Fake pine trees adorned with every conceivable color and shape of ornament occupied spaces throughout the building, and Christmas music was broadcast through the speakers. The atmosphere amongst her fellow journalists was contagious, and even the dour-faced administrators seemed to be more relaxed and joyful today. She only wished she could find some joy herself.

This would be the first Christmas that she would not be able to see or call or talk to her mother. They hadn't in fact been all that close over the last few years of her mother's life, which hurt Holly immeasurably. She took full responsibility for the lack of communication and she'd lost track of the times she'd wished she could roll back time and do things differently.

At the age of twenty-two, she wasn't meant to have so many regrets, and yet she did. Holly left home three years before, dissatisfied with her mother's stubborn refusal to discuss her father or his whereabouts. She'd never met the man and the only information her mother had been willing to impart was his name. Brian Sanders. Her mother had also admitted to Holly that the last time she'd seen him was when they had lived in Philadelphia.

Her mother, Sarah, had married Brian Sanders but divorced him after only two months. Brian had been extraordinarily lazy and became abusive whenever he drank. Sarah left him after finding out she was pregnant with Holly, and never looked back. Holly could understand her mother not wanting to stay married to such a man, but over the years she'd become increasingly desperate to find the man who'd fathered her, to ask him if he'd changed and why he'd never tried to contact her.

Her mother had been adamant that Brian didn't deserve her attention. Shortly after her nineteenth birthday, Holly and her mother had their final dispute over the issue. Holly had packed her belongings and headed to Philadelphia in search of the father who'd been missing all nineteen years of her life. Her mother was hurt by what she regarded as Holly's defection, but at the time Holly had been singularly focused on finding her father. She had not allowed herself the liberty of considering her mother's hurt feelings.

If she'd known how things would play out, she might

have done things differently. She had spent two months in Philadelphia looking for him before heading to the public library to carry out a name search. Her hopes had been to find a mention of Brian Sanders in the business pages of the newspaper. What she found instead was his obituary. He had died of liver cancer, caused by his predilection to live an alcoholic lifestyle, only ten days before she had arrived in Philadelphia.

Holly was devastated. She also discovered that her father was a frequent occupant at the local homeless shelter, his love for booze all too often winning out over his need to take care of himself. The woman at the shelter suggested she try and mend fences with her mother and get on with her life. Advice Holly had only partially taken.

In her mind she was sure she could have made a difference in her father's life, if only her mother had told her where to find him sooner. She had accused her mother as much. Her mother had remained resolutely silent and refused to discuss the matter. Their estrangement had perpetuated, and Holly had enrolled in night classes at the university and landed a job as a low-level journalist with a local newspaper.

Holly had acted out in accordance with her feelings of abandonment, without even realizing as much. It is natural for children to have emotional needs while growing up. These needs must be fulfilled, or the child will grow up to feel that she is not worthy of love or a rewarding life. While Holly had all her needs filled by her one present parent, including validation, approval, respect, acceptance, and understanding, she received none from her father. A single emotional need almost always takes center stage in every individual, and it is normally the one need which is least fulfilled. The child harbors what becomes a primary emotional need, which eventually affects her worth. Holly formed her own belief to explain why her one parent did not cater to her emotional needs. What developed from her natural explanation of the way in which she had grown up was a belief that she was not worthy of being loved or accepted. As such Holly spent her adolescent years trying to prove herself worthy. When her mother refused to explain away these harbored feelings of unworthiness, she had no reliable answers as to why her father was not around and did not want to know her. Holly eventually blamed her mother because the alternative would have been to blame herself for being unlovable. Holly started to resent her mother, seeing her as being judgmental. Holly eventually believed that her mother saw her as being the reason behind her father's absenteeism and her being alone since Holly's birth.

She'd placed the perfunctory phone calls to her mother on Christmas, Mother's Day, and her mom's birthday, but a wall had been thrown up between them and neither one was willing to swallow their pride. Holly still blamed her mother for keeping her away from her father, a man she would never get a chance to know now that he'd been dead almost three years. She had always felt like a piece of her was missing. Her mother had never understood her feelings on this and it had seemed that she had never tried to.

"Hey, Holly. Are you coming to the Christmas party

this weekend?" one of her co-workers called around the side of her cubicle.

Holly grimaced and then forced a half-smile. "I'm not sure quite yet."

"Oh, come on. Everyone's going to be there. You just have to come."

"I'll see," she agreed noncommittally. The last thing she wanted to do was attend a festive holiday party where everyone was smiling and having fun. That just wasn't her this year. Not now.

She turned to her desk and looked at the small photo of her mother taken when she was much younger. She picked it up and gently ran her fingertip around the bronze frame. "Mom... I can't believe you're really gone. I wish I would have done things differently. I wish I could have been there for you...with you..."

She had returned from covering the human-interest story five weeks earlier to find her editor waiting for her. The hospital had phoned him looking for Holly. It seemed her mother had suffered a heart attack. A heart attack which she had not survived. Holly was devastated. Her editor had shown immense compassion and driven her the thirty miles to the adjoining town for her to sign the paperwork and be allowed some measure of closure over her mother's passing.

Since the funeral held two days after Holly had visited the funeral home, Holly had been plagued by regrets. Her mother was far too young to die, at just barely forty, and it had been so sudden. She felt cheated out of the last three years of her life during which she had remained steadfastly and stubbornly angry over a man who was for all intents and purposes a stranger to her and who hadn't cared enough about her or her mother to stick around.

She'd found herself sitting silently for long periods of time, remembering her childhood and realizing how hard it had been on her mother to raise a young daughter on her own. Sarah was even more disadvantaged than most eighteen-year-old first-time mothers because she was raised Amish. She had only left her Amish Community after she met and married Brian Sanders.

Holly wasn't aware of just how hard her mother had found life in the Englisch world as a pregnant divorcée. Sarah successfully hid much of that from her daughter. After her mother's death however, Holly had researched the Amish lifestyle, and a clearer picture of the hardships her mother would have faced had started materializing in her understanding.

Her mother had never tried to return to the community in which she was raised, and Holly assumed that when she chose an Englischer over her family, they'd shunned her. By marrying Brian, she'd completely forsaken her family and friends. Her mother had never talked about her childhood, and Holly had always assumed her mother had no interest in recalling or dwelling upon that particular part of her life. After going through her mother's belongings on the day after the funeral, she'd realized how resolute her mother had always been never to complain about those aspects of life she felt she could not change.

"Day dreaming?" her editor asked, peering at her over the wall of her cubicle.

She straightened up and attempted to smile but failed miserably. "Not really."

"Uh huh. I don't buy that for a minute."

Holly shrugged her shoulders and then asked, "Did you need something?"

"For you to smile again, but I'll settle for a human-interest piece."

"Okay," Holly nodded. "Did you have something specific in mind?"

Her editor smiled, and she narrowed her eyes, knowing that grin meant he was about to meddle and there was nothing she could do to avoid it. Not if she wanted to keep her job. "I think our readers would love to hear how different cultures celebrate the holidays."

"Cultures?" she asked suspiciously.

"Yes. You know, Jewish, Asian, Amish…"

At his mention of the word Amish she knew where this was heading, and strangely enough, she found she didn't even want to fight him on it. "And you want me to research…?"

"The Amish, since you seem so fascinated with their culture of late."

Holly knew he'd seen her looking up information on the Amish culture more than once over the last few weeks. He'd asked her about it, and she'd told him in confidence that her mother had been raised Amish but had never spoken much about it or even tried to go back to visit her family.

He'd nodded and the next morning she'd found a list

of websites on her desk. Some were managed by former Amish while others were simply outsiders' observations. She'd found a wealth of information in those pages and had a growing desire to meet her mother's family and to see firsthand how they lived.

"I'll do it," she informed him before either could change their minds.

He looked at her, nodded once, and then strolled away, whistling a children's Christmas song. She stared after him for a moment and then called out, "I'm taking a field trip…"

"Take the entire week," he called back without turning around.

Holly smiled for the first time in what seemed like weeks, actually looking forward to this assignment. She now had a perfect reason to visit the local Amish communities, and she knew which one she would focus her efforts on—the one located in Lawrence County. Where her mother was born and raised.

Beliefs and Differences

Two days later...

Holly drove into the small town of Old Repton and used her phone's navigation to locate the bed and breakfast she would be living in during her time here. She'd spent the day before making arrangements and sifting through her mother's small box of keepsakes collected over the years.

Very little from her Amish past was to be found in the box, but Holly hadn't lost faith. She had a name and a location and, if her research into the Amish lifestyle was correct, her mother's family was probably still living in the same house, living in much the same way as before.

She looked around her as she parked the car, amazed at the festive atmosphere. She'd discovered during her research that the Amish were not the only inhabitants of Old Repton and had managed to find a way to coexist with their Englisch neighbors. According to some of the articles and websites she'd visited, the Amish maintained their lifestyle, and the Englisch who chose to live amongst them were very conservative and understanding. Her Airbnb would prove to be a prime example of that symbiosis.

The Airbnb was owned by an older Englischer couple who respected their Amish neighbors' beliefs and did their best to camouflage their differences. Holly appreciated the fact that these two cultures lived so close to one another and seemed to get along. Unfortunately, it also left her with more questions about her mother's reasons for leaving and never returning. She understood that her father was not part of the Amish community, but it seemed to her that they could have existed close by easy enough and for some reason had chosen not to. She hoped to better understand their reasons during the next week or so.

She slipped out of the car, locking the doors, and then turned away from the B&B and headed down the main sidewalk. She pushed her hands into the pockets of her wool coat, glad she'd brought it, along with her hat and gloves. A couple of inches of fresh snow had fallen during the previous night, and the Christmas lights scattered amongst some of the storefronts made it seem as if Christmas was upon them. A gentle breeze blew the snow around her ankles, making her even more thankful for fur-lined winter boots.

She paused for a moment in front of an obviously Amish store displaying a gorgeous quilt in the window. She glanced at the small drugstore next door and immediately noticed the contrasts. A further inspection of other storefronts distinguished the Amish from the other. Wreaths with large bows hung from the street lamps, garlands were strung up around entryways, and the Amish stores had placed candles in the windows. Some Englisch stores had tastefully decorated Christmas trees displayed inside, but the Amish storefronts were simple and mostly unadorned. She'd read online how the Amish considered Christmas trees, lights, and commercialization of the holiday season to be pagan. Christmas was all about Christ and remembering the birth of a baby two thousand years earlier, not Rudolph, snowmen, or Santa.

She'd celebrated Christmas as a child, but only now did her mother's reticence and discomfort with the holiday make more sense. She'd done her best to give her daughter a normal childhood, but she'd been completely out of her depth and in unfamiliar territory. A pang of guilt and sadness swamped Holly for a moment. *Mom had it so hard raising me in an unfamiliar place by herself, and towards the end, I was so ungrateful... I was a horrible daughter to her.*

Two children rushed by her, pulling her from her somber thoughts and into the jubilant atmosphere of the small town. Everywhere she looked, she saw people milling about with large smiles on their faces. She watched them as she walked along, wishing she had the right to join in their fun. A mixture of Amish and non-Amish walked the sidewalks, their children playing together in the fresh snow.

She found a vacant bench outside what appeared to be a local barbershop, where she took a seat to watch the people strolling by. Several groups of Amish women and men passed her, and she watched them with avid curiosity. The more she'd researched the culture, the more she'd found herself intrigued by their simple way of life. She was determined to learn whatever she could about them while she was here.

She longed for a connection to these people, and towards that end she pulled a photograph she'd found of her mother when she was much younger from her coat pocket. Her mother had been wearing a simple dress with her hair pinned back and secured atop her head, but the clothing wasn't Amish. She knew that because short buttons were clearly visible. How exactly does one make a shirt and hide the buttons? Another question she would love to have answered.

A snowball landed at her feet and she looked up from the photo to see to chagrined children rushing towards her, looking alarmed. They spoke to her rapidly in a language she guessed was Pennsylvania Dutch, which she could not understand.

She smiled at them and shook her head. "I'm sorry, but I don't understand you."

"They were apologizing for being rude and including you in their snowball fight without your permission," a smooth voice came from her left.

Holly turned her head and stared up into the gray eyes of a very handsome Amish man. His face showed that he wasn't a green youth while his unshaven face declared him unmarried. Why that thought made her pulse kick up, she wasn't quite sure, but the way in which he was looking at her brought her back to the fact that two red-faced little boys were standing in front of her awaiting her verdict.

She smiled at them. "That's okay. You didn't actually hit me with the snowball and on another day, I might actually join you, but not today."

The man standing to her left spoke to the boys who then nodded their heads before scampering off. He addressed her then in a thick accent, his English nearly perfect, with only the occasional Amish word sprinkled in. "They are gut kinner."

"I'm sure they meant no harm," she agreed with a nod. She'd done her research, as any good journalist would, and had acquainted herself with some basic Amish words. She was now very glad she had.

"You are visiting?" the young man inquired.

Holly nodded. "Yes, or should I say Jah?"

He grinned at her. "You speak our language?"

Holly smiled and shook her head. "Nee, I just taught myself a few words from the Internet."

He nodded his head. "The Internet. The Amish have no need of such devices. It is better to learn from doing." He looked up at a noise from down the street. "I must go. Enjoy your stay here."

Holly started to ask his name and introduce herself, but he was gone as quickly as he'd appeared. Shrugging, she stood up and headed towards the small quilt shop. *Might as well begin asking questions and see where it gets me.* She stepped inside and smiled as the owners came forward to greet her. She explained her reason for being there and how her mother had been raised Amish.

She showed them the photo and looked at them expectantly for any sign of recognition.

They looked at the photo, murmured between themselves, and then directed her to a shop further down the street where several members of long-standing Amish could be found. If anyone was able to help her, it would be them.

She thanked them and headed in that direction, hiding her disappointment that her first endeavor to find someone who had known her mother had failed. But she was a journalist at heart and loved solving a good mystery or riddle. Deciding to approach this task in that frame of mind, she hastened her steps and began her search in earnest.

It paid off, and the older woman manning the counter in the shop took the photo and nodded. "Jah. This is Sarah, is it not?"

Holly smiled for the first time in weeks and nodded. "My mother."

"I haven't seen your mamm for many years. Must be going on twenty now."

"Twenty-two to be exact. Do you know where I could find her family?"

"Her familye still manage one of the local dairy farms."

"A dairy farm?" she asked, never having given much thought to what her extended family might do for a living.

"Jah. If you want to meet some of your mamm's familye, there is a farmer's market tomorrow morning. Many of the Community bring their goods to be sold during this time as the Englisch are frequent visitors. This close to Christmas, most everyone should be in attendance."

"Tomorrow? I can do that. Do you know the name of their farm?" Holly asked, feeling hope blossom inside her chest at the prospect of meeting any member of her extended family.

"Just ask around, they will be found if that is their desire."

"But…" Holly began, confused because the shop owner had been so helpful up to this point.

"Your mamm left of her own accord and in doing so she cut herself off from her familye. It is for them to decide if they wish to know you, not me."

Holly slowly nodded her head before turning to leave the small shop. She had no desire to offend anyone, but just knowing that her mamm's familye was nearby sent a feeling of urgency through her. She was so close, and yet she had no control when it came to moving things forward. That would be up to them.

She headed to the bed and breakfast, intending to get settled and hopefully research this particular Amish community in more depth before the morning. She wanted to be as prepared as possible, should she be lucky enough to actually meet someone from her familye.

Christmas Blessings

The next morning...

Holly stepped inside the barn and was momentarily transfixed by the number of Amish there. Wooden tables, carts laden with a variety of produce and preserved foods, colorful quilts, and wooden furniture were displayed in neat rows. It was a little difficult for her to distinguish between the Amish as individuals since they were all dressed alike in plain fabric dresses of royal blue, navy blue, black, and varying shades of brown. The men wore dark denim trousers with a double placket on the front held up by suspenders, and topped by a traditional felt hat, while the women, except the very youngest children, all wore either white or black prayer kapps.

Holly smiled at her mental use of the Amish terms. Her research had intrigued her, and she'd challenged herself to use the Dutch derivatives as often as possible while in Old Repton.

She wandered down the aisles, looking at the various offerings and searching for anyone who might resemble her mamm or appear to be from a working dairy farm. So engrossed was she in her search that she hadn't realized she was frowning with concentration until a familiar voice spoke above her head.

"We meet again."

Holly whirled around and looked up into the gray eyes of the mann she'd met the day before. "Oh, hello."

"Gutentag. You wish to buy something?"

Holly shook her head. "Not really, I was just wandering a little."

The mann looked at her with curiosity and then shook his head. "I think you do not tell the whole truth. You seemed to be looking for something in particular."

Holly was amazed and huffed out a short laugh. "You would be right. Are you a mind reader?"

He smiled and shook his head. "Nee, just observant." He looked over her shoulder for a moment and then returned his attention to her. "My name is Evan Miller."

Holly extended her hand, and then let it drop when he merely looked at it. Strange and a bit rude she thought. She believed the Amish did shake hands? Maybe because she was a stranger and a woman? In her world she would have been offended, but she wasn't in her world and differences of cultural practice had to be accepted. She decided to ignore the snub. She rubbed her palm on her thigh and then smiled. "I'm Holly Sanders. Do you live around here?"

"All of my life," he confirmed, once again looking

over her shoulder. She opened her mouth to speak again but stopped when he turned away from her.

"Excuse me for a moment."

She watched as he strolled across the aisle and took hold of the hand of a little girl. He squatted down to be at eye-level with her and seemed to be talking solemnly. She threw her little body against his and he hugged her close. He soothed her for a moment and then picked her up to carry her to where Holly still stood waiting.

"I apologize. Holly, this is my niece, Becca Yoder. Becca, this nice lady is Holly."

Holly looked at the little girl and then smiled. "Hello Becca."

The little girl simply stared back at her with big brown eyes full of too much sorrow for one so young.

Evan murmured in the little girl's ear, but she shook her head and buried her face in his neck. "I'm sorry. Becca is…well, she's a bit shy."

Holly nodded, thinking he'd meant to say something more, but had held back because of the little girl. An older girl approached just then. "Evan, is it okay if I take Becca over to sit with the sheep?"

Evan looked for a response from his niece, but when none was forthcoming, he sighed and then set her down on the ground. "Becca, go with Miriam for a bit. I'll come get you in twenty minutes."

Becca took the other girl's hand and allowed herself to be led away, her expression never changing at all.

Evan watched after her, revealing a look of helplessness for only a moment before he corrected it. "Becca's had a rough time in recent months." He turned back to

Holly. "Her mamm was my older schweschder. Ruth. She and her husband were killed in a house fire a few months back and Becca came to live with me. She hasn't spoken a word since the fire."

Holly's heart broke for the little girl. "That's horrible."

"I have to believe it was Gott's will, but there are times when my faith is tested."

Holly looked at him in confusion. "You think Gott wanted her parents to die in a fire?"

Evan shook his head. "Nee, that is not what I meant or think at all. The Amish believe that Gott has a purpose for each of our lives. We are not to question it but should trust Him in all that we do. I don't why Ruth was taken from this earthly existence so soon, but I believe that we will be reunited one day in Heaven. Until that time, I will look after Becca to the best of my ability."

"That's a lot of responsibility," Holly told him, thinking about the information she'd discovered about her own mamm and how hard being a single parent had been.

Evan smiled. "This I know. But, enough about my troubles. What is Holly Sanders looking for?"

"Answers," she replied before she could think about her response. She looked up when she realized what she'd done, but Evan didn't seem too concerned by her response.

"Well, answers can be easy to obtain, but first one must know the question."

Holly nodded, and then blurted out, "My mamm was raised here."

"In Pennsylvania?" Evan asked.

Holly shook her head. "Right here in Old Repton. She was Amish and left when she married an Englischer."

Evan's face closed down briefly and then he seemed to catch himself and he slowly asked, "What was your mamm's name?"

"Sarah Bontrager."

Evan was silent for a moment and then asked, "Is your mamm here with you?"

Holly shook her head. "She passed away a few months ago. I knew she was Amish, but she never wanted to talk about that period of her life. I was hoping to find her familye by coming here."

Evan looked off across the barn for a moment and then seemed to come to a decision. "I will help you do this."

"You will?" she asked, surprise evident in her voice.

"Jah. Everyone should know their familye. Your mamm made a decision to leave here, but that doesn't mean that she became any less her parents' dochder. I personally do not like the way the elders of the past handled these types of situations, and while things have changed only a tiny bit in the past twenty years, kinner who choose to leave the Community are no longer shunned as they were back then. Unfortunately, your mamm was probably very aware that she would be cut off entirely from her familye when she left."

Holly nodded. "I don't know much about that time of her life, but I was hoping to maybe find some friends or anyone who might have remembered her. I would really like to know more about my heritage."

"Heritage is a gut thing. I will make some inquiries on your behalf. Will you be staying in town?"

Holly gave him the name of the Airbnb she was booked into and he smiled. "They are very nice people and you will enjoy your stay there. I will send word to you there if I find anything out."

Holly bit her bottom lip. "Thank you. Why are you helping me?" He was a very good looking young man, and Holly acknowledged that she found him very attractive even though he was Amish.

Evan smiled at her. "I'm helping you because I like you."

Holly raised a brow. "You like me?"

"Jah. I've never met anyone like you and would like to learn more about your world."

"What do you want to know?" she asked him, willing to tell him about her world if he was going to help her locate her familye.

Evan grinned at her. "We will have to save that conversation for a later date. I need to retrieve Becca and get her home for lunch. Holly, have a gut day and I will speak to you again soon."

Holly nodded and watched him stride away. She spent the rest of the morning wandering around the small town before returning to the bed and breakfast. The Marlows owned the five-bedroom place and loved making it as homely as possible for their guests. She found Mrs. Marlow baking cookies in the kitchen when she returned.

"Come and join me, dear, and tell me what you've been up to today."

Holly did so, helping cut out and then decorate sugar cookies in a variety of Christmas shapes and sizes. She told Mrs. Marlow about meeting Evan and his offer to help, at which Mrs. Marlow merely smiled and told her what a fine young man Evan Miller was. She was lucky to have met him and have him on her side. As she climbed the stairs to her assigned room several hours later, she found herself unable to stop thinking about the gray eyes, dark wavy hair, and gentle nature of the mann.

The way he handled his mute niece's silence spoke volumes, and Holly was once again reminded that it was easy to tell the measure of a mann by how he treated small children and animals. Evan Miller was indeed a good man and Holly figured Becca was blessed to have him in her life.

The Boy Next Door

The next afternoon...

While Holly waited for Evan to make contact with her, she busied herself talking with others in the community, as well as helping Mrs. Marlow bake Christmas cookies and goodies for the annual Christmas Program the children would be putting on on Christmas Eve night. The Marlows had all of the traditional holiday adornments, including a large tree with sparkling lights and glass ornaments. Inside the small establishment, it was easy to forget that she was in the heart of Amish country.

But outside in the town, the differences were stark. Holly found herself intrigued with the plainer decorations she found in the Amish shops. Stars and evergreen wreaths with handmade bows and berries seemed to be the most common decorations, if indeed anything at all. Nothing flashy, and nothing that wasn't completely handmade. No strings of lights, no Christmas trees... even the wrapping paper they used was plain and unadorned. It seemed the simple life extended to all facets of their existence. Now that the days were shorter, they even used oil lanterns to light their small shops.

She accompanied Mrs. Marlow late afternoon the next day to deliver her contribution to the Christmas program, and was enjoying the song the children were singing, when she noticed a young girl sitting all alone on a bench by the wall. When she recognized her as Becca Yoder, she looked around for her uncle. Not finding him, Holly made her way over to the little girl and sat down beside her.

"Hello, Becca. Do you remember me? We met in the barn yesterday. You were with your Uncle Evan?"

Becca looked up at her but refused to speak. Holly tried again. "Is your uncle here?" then remembered that the girl had not spoken for a long time.

Becca gave a short shake of her head and then turned her attention back to the front of the building where the other children were practicing their poems and songs.

Holly was concerned and felt compassion for the little girl. She paused for a moment and then asked, "You don't like to sing? I bet you have a beautiful voice."

Becca didn't respond, and Holly thought maybe she was being ignored, when she noticed the little girl's fingers were keeping time with the music. *She's heartbroken, but not lost. She probably loved to sing before...*

Mrs. Marlow joined them and leaned down to give the little girl a hug that wasn't returned. "Hi Becca, how are you today?" She paused to wait for a response and then continued as if one had been given. "Well, I'm doing fine as well."

Holly watched the interaction, making a mental note to ask Mrs. Marlow about the little girl's silence when they were alone. "Is someone watching her?" she asked instead.

"The Amish children are all practicing for the Christmas program. I'm sure her teacher is around here somewhere. They'll head back to their homes anytime now."

Holly nodded and then stood up. "I didn't want to just leave her sitting here if she was lost or something of that sort."

"She's not lost, she's just grieving," Mrs. Marlow told her quietly. "Becca, tell your uncle hello from me. I'll bring you to dinner one day this week." She looked at Holly and gestured towards the doors. "She'll be fine."

Holly was torn, but then again, the little girl was not her responsibility. She followed Mrs. Marlow back to her car, relaxing when she spied Evan driving a buggy into the parking area. "Looks like Evan just arrived to pick her up."

Mrs. Marlow smiled. "Evan is doing a remarkable job. It's not every day a young mann of twenty-six takes on the responsibility of raising his five-year-old niece. He never even got to grieve the loss of his schweschder."

Holly gave her a strange look at the use of the Amish word.

"When you've lived around here long enough, you start using the Amish words occasionally, especially when talking about them."

Holly nodded completely understanding; she had a friend that went to university in Oxford in England, and when she returned she had a British twang to her speech. Holly continued the conversation as though the comment about the Amish words had not even been made. "It must be hard on them both. Does he not have anyone to help?" She didn't want to think of Evan as having a wife and tried to convince herself that wasn't why she'd asked the question.

Mrs. Marlow shook her head. "His parents were older and died some years back. He works the land that has been in his family's possession for decades."

"Evan's a farmer?" Holly asked, soaking up the information and trying to reconcile the Evan she'd barely begun to know with the one Mrs. Marlow was describing.

"Oh yes, they farmed the land for years. Generations to be honest. But they both died a few years back, a few months apart from one another. It was as though one couldn't live without the other, if ever there was a case of death by a broken heart then that was it. And then the house fire happened and Evan's schweschder was taken away as well. I've been amazed at how well he's adjusted to having young Becca living with him."

"He mentioned that she hasn't talked since the accident?" Holly asked, becoming even more interested in learning about Evan Miller. He had those boy-next-door good looks that so many of her friends had gushed over while growing up. The fact that he'd put his own plans aside and taken in his niece was amazing. She knew and worked with a number of single young men in their latter twenties, and she couldn't imagine any of them putting aside their own lives to care for a little girl.

"Becca was trapped by the fire and a neighbor managed to get her out before the smoke got to her. Evan tried to save Elizabeth, his sister, and her husband Noah, but the flames were too strong. I know he feels guilty and that looking after the child is his duty."

"She must have been so scared," Holly murmured, trying to imagine all the little girl had suffered while waiting to be rescued.

Mrs. Marlow nodded her head. "I cannot imagine the horror myself, sends shivers down my spine. I'm sure the trauma has caused her to be mute. If she had been outside of the community then she would probably have seen a psychologist by now, but as you know the Amish have their ways. Bishop Miller believes she will speak again once her mind has a chance to heal."

"I hope so, she's a beautiful little girl."

Mrs. Marlow smiled. "But in the Amish world beauty is vanity and to be avoided lest it corrupts the soul."

"You sound very knowledgeable about all things Amish," Holly commented, again forgetting where she was.

"Of course! I was raised around the Amish. They are a simple people and mostly misunderstood by those in the outside world. Englisch is what they call outsiders, whether they are actually of English descent or not."

"I read that online. I would imagine that it would be very difficult to leave here and have to adjust to the world in which I live. I just keep wondering why my mamm would have done such a thing."

"Many people, even Amish youngsters, think the grass is greener on the other side. They are tempted by what they don't have, and sometimes it gets the better of them. In your mamm's case, I imagine she was struggling with rebellion and encountered an Englischer who thought he was doing her some big favor by taking her away from the only life she knew. She wouldn't have been the first and she certainly won't be the last."

Holly considered that for a moment. "My parents didn't stay married very long. According to my mother, my daed was a drunkard and abusive. I don't think she realized his true nature until they were already married. She only stayed with him for a short time and left because of me."

Mrs. Marlow was quiet for a moment and then suggested, "When Evan talks to your family and you get to meet them, keep an open mind. Things might not be as you assume."

Holly started to ask for an explanation, but they had arrived at the bed and breakfast and Mrs. Marlow was already out of the vehicle and heading for the kitchen door.

"Well, I'm not sure what she meant by that, but keep an open mind I most certainly will do."

Realizing she was talking to herself out loud, she exited the vehicle and headed for her bedroom. She'd do a bit more research on the Amish and their lifestyle, in the hope that one day soon she would be able to meet some of her mamm's familye and not embarrass herself in the process of getting to know them. She wanted to fit in so badly, and just the prospect of knowing she had relatives who were alive put a smile upon her face.

Maybe I'm not all alone in this world after all, she thought.

Being Amish

Three days later...

"Holly, Evan, and Becca are coming to dinner this evening. I was wondering if you would mind helping me in the kitchen?" Mrs. Marlow asked as she sipped her first cup of tea a few days later.

"I would be happy to, but I have to confess, I do better with a microwave than a stove top."

Mrs. Marlow chuckled. "You'll do fine. I'll talk you through everything. I'm surprised that your mamm didn't teach you how to cook, being Amish and all."

Holly shook her head. "She worked all the time. I didn't realize how hard things must have been for her once she left my daed. She was a waitress, and I can remember she often worked the evening shift because the tips were better.

"She would pick me up from school and I would spend the evening in the backroom watching the small television and doing my homework. She would check on me often, and I grew up thinking it was normal to spend so much time away from your home."

Holly sighed and made a face. "I never realized the sacrifices she made for me until it was too late. I was in high school before I realized I had started to want what other kids had. I thought that if I could just find my daed maybe things would be all right and she wouldn't have to work so much."

Mrs. Marlow joined her at the table. "Did you ever find him?"

Holly nodded. "In the pages of the obituaries. He passed away not too long before I went looking for him. I blamed her, of course. I thought I could save him, but I've since come to realize he didn't want to be saved. He lived his life by his choice."

"That must have been a hard discovery."

"A little. It was harder when I found out that she'd died from a heart attack before I had the chance to tell her I was sorry for putting all the blame on her. I still regret that."

Mrs. Marlow made a tsking sound and then stood up. "Regrets steal the future. Come into the kitchen and I will show you how to make bread. That is sure to get your mind thinking about other things."

"Bread?"

Mrs. Marlow looked at her and then laughed. "Bread. Trust me, every woman should know how to bake a decent loaf of bread."

Holly followed her with a smile. "I did tell you I can't cook, right?"

"Oh ye of little faith. Everyone can cook with a little help."

Seven hours later...

Holly heard the front door open and she had to make a concerted effort to slow down as she headed downstairs. Evan was taking Becca's woolen coat off when she reached the bottom of the stairs, and he looked up at her and smiled warmly.

"Gutennacht, Holly. Something smells amazing."

"That would be the bread that Holly made earlier today."

Evan grinned at Mrs. Marlow and then smiled at Holly. "You made bread?"

Holly blushed and nodded. "Mrs. Marlow decided I needed to learn how to cook."

"Cooking is a gut thing and Mrs. Marlow does it well. Learning from her is also a gut thing."

Holly smiled and then addressed Becca. "How are you?" Becca didn't respond but Holly was prepared for that. "Do you want to sit with me while dinner is cooking? I found some coloring books and crayons in a drawer upstairs. I thought maybe you could help me color a picture."

Becca looked at her shyly for a moment, and then directed her eyes back to the ground. "Holly, I'm sorry..." Evan began.

"Don't be," she assured Evan with a shake of her head. She walked over and extended her hand to the little girl. "Come on, Becca. We'll let Uncle Evan keep

Mrs. Marlow entertained. Mr. Marlow is out back cutting firewood."

Holly held her breath until the little girl slowly put her fingers in Holly's hand. She nodded once and then walked the little girl down the hallway to a wooden table on which was a coloring book and a box of crayons.

Holly helped her get seated on the high chair and then she opened the book and began slowly turning the pages. "You tell me when you want me to stop. You can color the right page and I'll color the left one."

Becca made no comment, but when Holly was about halfway through the book, her little hand suddenly came off her lap and landed on a picture of two kittens playing with a ball of yarn on one side, and a cat cleaning her paw on the other.

"Oh, you like kittens?" Holly asked. She waited for Becca to respond, pleased when the little girl nodded once. "I've never had a kitten." She kept up a one sided conversation about cats and kittens while she opened the box of crayons and spilled them across the table. Becca picked up a black crayon and began coloring one of the kittens.

Holly watched her out the corner of her eye and thought things were going well until she saw the first teardrop hit the coloring book. She looked over to see tears flowing down Becca's face, her mouth turned down in sorrow as she silently cried.

"Oh, sweetie! I didn't intend to make you cry." Holly put down the crayon and pulled the little girl unresisting onto her lap. She wrapped her arms around her and rocked back and forth. "It's okay. I know things seem bad right now, but Uncle Evan loves you."

"I miss Smokey," a teeny tiny voice mumbled against her neck.

Holly's breath stalled even as her heart shouted for joy. She spoke! "Who is Smokey, sweetie?"

"My kitten. He burned up like…" The gravity of her words stopped her as fresh tears assailed her. This time, not so quietly. Holly sensed Evan's presence before she saw him step into the room.

His eyes took in the scene before him and he mouthed, "What happened?"

Holly felt her own tears spill over as she held the sobbing little girl in her arms. "We were coloring kittens and she started crying. She misses Smokey."

Knowing entered Evan's eyes and his shoulders sagged. "Her kitten."

"Jah," Holly answered him, the use of the Amish term falling from her lips so easily.

Evan gave her a smile and moved to sit down behind them, placing a tender hand on his niece's head. "Becca, do you miss your kitten?"

Becca's sobs had eased somewhat, and she nodded her head but refused to talk to her uncle, even though he tried repeatedly. Finally, after ten minutes or so, he stood up. "I'll let you two finish what you were doing. Dinner's almost ready I believe."

"Evan…" Holly called to him, not knowing what to do to correct what she saw as a problem. His niece who hadn't spoken a word since the fire, had spoken to her but wouldn't talk to him.

Evan smiled at her tenderly and shook his head. "Don't apologize. I am so grateful that she has chosen to speak again, I don't care if it is not to me yet. Denke, Holly. You are an answer to my prayers."

Holly shook her head. "I'm not an answer to anyone's prayer."

Evan stepped back towards her and squatted to eye-level. "You are mine. Denke."

After he left the room, Holly spent a few minutes picking up the spilled crayons while Becca quietly told her about the ten-week old kitten that had perished in the fire along with her parents. Holly knew that kinner didn't process death in the same way as adults, and it seemed that she was accepting of the fact that her mamm and daed were now in Heaven with Gott but was heartbroken over the loss of her pet.

Several hours later, Becca had fallen asleep on the couch, the unfinished picture of the kittens held tightly in her hands. Holly watching her and then realized that Evan was looking at her from across the room.

"Would you care to take a short walk with me?" he asked.

"Sure," Holly nodded. "Just let me grab a coat. It's chilly outside."

"Jah. More snow is expected over the next couple of days I'm told. But Gott will decide if it is so or not."

They walked around the gardens around the back of the house, a high moon lighting their path. "I'm really sorry that Becca won't talk to you," she began again.

Evan stopped and turned her to face him, his hands resting gently on her shoulders. "Please don't apologize. She's talking and crying. Do you know, she hasn't cried once?"

Holly nodded. "She told me without any sadness that her parents were with God but she cried over the kitten. Is there any possible way that she get another kitten?" She realized how she might sound and backtracked. "Sorry, I know that's not my place to even suggest…"

"Nee. Stop apologizing for caring. I'm not sure if anyone has kittens around here at this time of year. Mostly, kittens are born to barn cats and must be removed and tamed as soon as they are weaned to make good house pets."

"Well, maybe in the Spring she could get another one?"

"Jah, maybe in the Spring." He took a deep breath and told her the big news that he had for her. "I wanted to let you know I was able to track down your mamm's parents and a few of her school friends. I'm sorry it took so long, but there are so many Amish around here and with everyone having the same few surnames it becomes very difficult at times to work out who is who."

Holly smiled broadly. "Really? Don't apologize. I'm just so glad you managed to track people down. Her parents are still alive?" Grandparents she couldn't help but to think, *the Grandparents that I've never met.*

"Jah. They own a dairy farm a short way away. I spoke to the bishop yesterday and he thinks they would welcome a visit from you."

Holly's wish seemed about to come true, and she had Evan to thank for it. Before she could think about the inappropriateness of her gesture, she threw her arms around him and hugged him. "Thank you. Denke. However else you want me to say it."

Evan held himself rigidly for a long moment, and just as she realized that what she'd done wasn't acceptable in his culture, his body relaxed, and his arms came around her back and he hugged her in return. His voice was a bit scratchy and soft when he murmured above her head, "You are very welcome. I can't take you there tomorrow, but I could do so the day after. If that is acceptable?"

Holly pulled herself away from him, feeling the heat stain her cheeks when she realized just how safe and right it had felt to be in his arms. *He's Amish and they don't hug like that. He probably only hugged you back because he didn't know what else to do.*

"I...the day after tomorrow? You will drive me there?"

"Well, in my buggy, jah. I will drive you there. Becca will need to come along of course."

"That won't be a problem." She went on to think to herself, *in fact, having the little girl along will help keep my wandering thoughts about how handsome you are at bay.*

"Gut! I will come by for you around 8 o'clock."

"In the morning?" she asked, dismay in her voice and showing on her face.

Evan chuckled. "Jah, in the morning. I should be done with the morning chores by 7. I will be here at 8 o'clock."

Holly had never been a morning person. At the office her work colleges knew better than to approach her before she had sunk her second cup of coffee of the day. But this was something special, it was time to break the habits of a lifetime. Holly nodded her head. "Fine. I'll be ready to go."

They walked back to the Marlow's place and slipped as quietly as possible back inside. Evan looked down at Becca, still sleeping where they had left her.

"Denke, Holly," Evan said, "for the way you have taken to Becca. It means a lot."

Holly blushed and nodded her head silently. Evan gave her one more glance and then headed for the front door. Mr. Marlow was just coming back inside with another armful of wood for the fireplaces and Evan held the door open for him. "Goodnight, Evan."

"Gutennacht, Mr. Marlow. Dinner was very good as always."

"We enjoyed having you and getting to see Becca. Drive safe."

"We will. Holly, I will see you the day after tomorrow. Sleep well."

A Day Blessed by Gott

Two days later...

Holly was nervous. Evan had picked her up half an hour before, and Becca had offered her the tiniest of smiles but no words. They were now driving down the small street of the neighboring town where her grandparents lived. Evan had suggested they stop at a local bakery for breakfast before getting directions to the dairy farm where her mamm had grown up.

Holly hadn't had much experience with horses and she half expected the horse to bolt at any moment taking them with him. But Evan and his horse seemed at one with each other and as the ride continued she tried to relax.

He parked the buggy next to several identical buggies different only in the appearance of the horses they were drawn by. "Let me help you down," he offered, coming around and holding on to her elbow as she stepped from the buggy. Becca followed her out and then reached for her hand.

Holly took it and smiled down at her. "Are you hungry?" Becca nodded, but once again remained verbally silent. "So am I."

Evan escorted them to the door and, as Holly and Becca stepped inside, they were assailed by the smell of butter and sugar and the sound of the clanging of the bell overhead. Wooden floors creaked underfoot as they walked towards the small counter, and Holly deeply inhaled the smell of fresh pastries and hot coffee. "It smells delicious."

"Welcome, what can I get for you today?" a middle-aged woman behind the counter asked in broken English.

"I'm going to have one of those cinnamon twists," Holly requested before she squatted down next to Becca. "What kind of pastry do you like to eat, sweetie?"

Becca was eyeing the various offerings and eventually pointed to a donut covered in colored sprinkles. Holly smiled and nodded. "That looks wonderful." She informed the clerk of Becca's choice and watched while Evan made his selection, also ordering a glass of milk for his niece and two cups of coffee for her and himself.

"We're going to find a place to sit down. Is my grandparents' place far from here?"

Evan looked at her and then shook his head. "I don't really know, but I'll ask." He turned back to the clerk. "Excuse me, but do you happen to know where the Bontrager dairy farm is located?"

The clerk eyed them both suspiciously and asked, "Are they expecting you?"

Evan shook his head. "Nee, but this is a surprise I think they will like." He gestured towards Holly. "This is their grossdochder."

"What?! Who was your mamm?" the clerk asked, coming around the counter in haste.

Holly met the woman's eyes. "Sarah Bontrager."

"Oh my!" She looked Holly up and down and then hugged her tightly. "Welcome, Holly. You look like your mamm when she was much younger. How is she? Is she with you?"

Holly stepped back and shook her head. "Nee. She died a few months ago."

The woman's eyes teared up. "Oh, I would have so liked to have talked with her again. But I'm forgetting my manners. My name is Dawn and your mamm and I were best friends until she left." She called into the back of the bakery, "Anna! Abby! Sarah Bontager's dochder is here."

"Sarah Bontrager?" another middle-aged woman asked, appearing out of the kitchen wearing an apron over her dress with her hands covered in flour. "The one that left the community?"

"Jah! Come and meet her," Dawn urged them both.

Holly found herself suddenly surrounded by voices and it wasn't until a tiny hand pushed its way into her own that she remembered Evan and Becca were with her.

"Sweetie, let's get you settled. Excuse me, but Becca needs to sit down and eat. Maybe you could talk with us while she does that?"

Dawn nodded and grabbed a tray and their selected items. Abby and Anna shook their heads. "We have work to do. Please come and see us again. We would love to know what your mamm did after leaving here."

Dawn returned and after Becca was settled, she pulled up another chair. "Is this your dochder?" clearly confused about the Amish dress that Becca was wearing.

Holly shook her head, part of her wishing for the first time in her adult life that she could say a child was hers. She'd not really given any thought to having children but being around Becca and getting to know Evan had changed that.

"Nee, she is Evan's niece. He is raising her in the absence of her parents who are in Heaven now." She spoke the words softly, not wanting to upset the little girl needlessly.

Dawn looked at Evan and then smiled. "That is good of you. So, your familye is going to be so surprised."

Holly nodded. "I hope it will be a good one."

"It will be. They were upset when Sarah decided to live amongst the Englisch, but Brian would never have fit in here. He held everything that was Amish in great disdain and often told your mamm how idiotic he found our lifestyle. He called it bizarre and controlling."

"You met my father?" Holly asked a little taken back, she wasn't expecting to have come into contact with someone who had met her father.

Dawn nodded her head. "I have to confess, I never liked him. After your mother left here, I snuck away a few times and called her on the phone number she'd given me. She sounded terribly unhappy. Brian wasn't the man she thought he was, but she'd already left and the bishop at the time was a very hard mann who would have never allowed her back without making her grovel and embarrassing her. She didn't deserve to be treated like that, so she made the decision to live in the Englisch world.

"It was very hard for her and I wish we could have kept in touch, but the bishop discovered that she and I had kept in contact and my parents forbade me from speaking with her again."

Holly nodded. "I'm sure she would have liked to have kept in contact with you, even though she never talked about her childhood."

"It was probably too painful. She gave up everything for you."

"For me?" Holly asked.

"Jah. She left Brian when she found out she was pregnant with you and he wanted to get steps to…" she paused, not wanting the say the words, "you know what I mean!"

Holly gasped, fully understanding her meaning. "She never told me that."

Dawn gave her a sad smile. "She wouldn't have, it was not her way. She suffered and endured many hardships, but she did it out of love for you."

Holly felt tears sting her eyes and then noticed that Becca and Evan were both finished and waiting for her. "My friends are done, and I shouldn't keep them waiting any longer. Evan brought me here to meet my grandparents."

Dawn grinned. "Would it be rude of me to ask if I

might come as well? I would to see the look on their faces. Oh, and you have a whole bunch of aunts and uncles and cousins and nieces and nephews…the Bontrager familye is very large."

"My mamm had siblings?" Holly asked, a little taken back. She hadn't given much thought to an extended family beyond her grandparents. The fact that her mother had never mentioned them was strange. But she didn't fully understand the dynamics. If her siblings had disapproved then maybe the parting between them was worse than with her parents?

Dawn smiled. "She had seven bruders and schweschders, all of whom have their own familyes now. Are you ready for such a big reunion?"

"Oh." She nodded eagerly. "Jah. Bitte."

"I can see you're already trying to fit in. Where are you staying?"

Holly told her about the Airbnb and then Dawn shook her head. "Nee, you should stay with me. I have an extra bedroom that is not being used and you will be close enough to walk over and visit your familye anytime you want."

"Really?" she asked, thrilled that an Amish woman would allow her to stay with her but then she looked at Evan and realized that if she stayed with Dawn, she might not see Evan again. "Can I think about that and get back to you?"

"Of course. Let me tell the others I'm leaving for a bit and I will lead the way with my own buggy. This is truly a day blessed by Gott."

The Perfect Day

H er first meeting with her grandparents was better than she could have ever hoped for. They welcomed her with open arms and word spread quickly amongst the neighbors. Before midday, she'd been introduced to so many people, she knew she'd never be able to remember all their names.

Evan and Becca had been welcomed just as warmly, but when the other kinner had urged Becca to go play with them, she'd sidled up next to Holly and refused to leave her or Evan's side. By 3 o'clock, Becca was sleeping against Evan's shoulder and Holly knew it was time for her to leave.

"I cannot thank you enough for welcoming me so warmly. I wish I'd been able to meet you all sooner."

"No regrets, Holly. Your mamm did what she thought was best, and at the time, the only option really available to her was to leave our Community and make her way in the Englisch world. Denke for coming to find us. After all of these years, Gott has finally heard our prayers and answered them," her grandmother said with a warm smile that reminded her of her mother.

Evan smiled and then whispered to her, "See, you're someone else's answer to prayer."

Holly blushed and then hugged her newfound family, with promises to return soon. She was still mulling over Dawn's invitation to stay with her, and her grandparents had offered her the use of her mamm's old bedroom as well. She decided she wasn't going to make any decisions today but would sleep on it before choosing the best path.

She remained silent during the trip back to Old Repton and the Marlow's place, with Becca curled up on her side asleep, her head in Holly's lap. "She's very tired."

"She's had an exciting few days. Did she speak to you again today?"

Holly shook her head. "Nee, but things were very chaotic with so many new people to meet. I was overwhelmed at times today, I can only imagine how it must have been for her. Denke for bringing me here today. I never dreamed things would go this well."

"You are very welcome. I prayed that Gott would help prepare their hearts for your arrival."

"You do that a lot? Pray?"

"Jah. Prayer has brought me great comfort over the years. Especially recently. Do you never pray?" he asked in the gathering darkness.

Holly was quiet for a long moment. "Not as much as I should. My mother read her Bible a lot and prayed. We went to a small church, but she was always very quiet and didn't really want to get too involved. I never really thought about the change it must have been for her."

"I imagine an Englisch church was much different than an Amish service. Here we gather at the homes of our neighbors every few weeks. There are no musical instruments, and the sermons can last a while—over an hour isn't considered strange. We have two of them every service."

"Two sermons? Oh my," laughed Holly, thinking about how she might have fallen asleep in some when she was a child. If she had been forced to sit through two then she would never have kept her eyes open.

"Jah. Things are very different here."

"I can see that," she laughed again, pointing at the horse.

But then she thought she better get an issue that had been playing on her mind off her chest. "I'm sorry if my hug the other day made you uncomfortable."

Evan was quiet for a moment. "While it is true that unmarried Amish women do not hug unmarried menner, your hug was…" He stopped, as if at a loss for words. She gave him a moment, but when he didn't start speaking again, she tried to fill in the blank for him. "My hug was awful?"

Evan shook his head. "Nee. It was nice."

Holly felt her heartrate increase. Was it possible that Evan was as attracted to her as she was to him? That would be nice, but then again, he was Amish. How would that work exactly? It wouldn't would it?

"So, you weren't offended?"

"Nee."

She decided to test the waters. "So if I was to do it again, you would…?"

Evan glanced at her and then sighed. "It would depend. If there was a reason for the hug, I would probably return it. Unless the bishop was somewhere near, and then I would receive a stern lecture. That is something I would like to avoid at all costs."

"The bishop would lecture you?" Holly asked, teasing him just a bit.

"Jah," he laughed, throwing his head back as though it were the funniest thing he had ever heard. "That would be worse than when my daed would lecture my schweschders and I."

"I'll try to contain my hugs to when no one else is around," she teased him, realizing that she was already looking forward to the next time she had a proper excuse to hug him. In the Amish world, that time probably didn't exist but, in this instance, she decided she could borrow some of her Englischer upbringing.

"So, what did you think about Dawn's offer of staying with her?" Evan asked in the quiet of the buggy.

"I really enjoyed talking with her, but I'm not sure I want to stay with her. It didn't take us too long to travel here, and I'm very comfortable with the Marlows right now. Besides, I owe my editor a story in the next few days about my perceived differences between what I think of as Christmas and how the Amish celebrate the holiday."

"You are a writer?" enquired Evan, feeling a little stupid that he hadn't even asked such a basic question as to what she did for a living.

"A journalist for a newspaper. My editor knew I was interested in learning more about my mamm's familye and I personally think he came up with this assignment to give me an excuse to visit here."

"That would be very nice of him," Evan murmured. "Do you have enough information to write your article?"

"I do. Mrs. Marlow and some of the shopkeepers were very helpful. I've actually enjoyed getting to know them and I have realized that by taking the commercialism out of Christmas, one can more easily remember the reason for the holiday."

"Without the birth of Christ, there is no Christmas," Evan concluded for her.

"Exactly. Back in Philadelphia, the department stores begin decorating for Christmas before Halloween, and it seems that everything is about Santa, reindeer, and presents. It was refreshing to hear some of the shopkeepers' kids explain the true meaning of Christmas and to hear them talk about how much fun they have playing board games with their friends and family. I wish more kinner could experience that."

"You sound like you enjoy being here."

Holly nodded. "You sound surprised?"

"I am, honestly. Learning to live without all of the modern conveniences the Englisch world has to offer has got to be hard."

"How do you know about the modern conveniences?" she asked.

"I spent a few months during Rumspringa living amongst the Englisch and I made the decision to come back here. Life is so much simpler here where there is plenty of time to enjoy the little things in life. In the city, the little things became unnoticeable and that saddened me."

Holly knew exactly what he meant and nodded her head. "There seems to be a lot less stress with your way of life."

"Stress is bad for the mind and the body. Do you plan to still be here at Christmas?" he asked as he pulled into the driveway of the B&B.

"I don't know. I don't really have anyone to spend it with back home."

"Would you consider having Christmas dinner with Becca and me?" Evan asked. "Mrs. Marlow has promised to cook, and several neighbors will be joining us as well. I'm sure if Becca were awake and in a speaking mood she would want you to stay. It's only another eight days."

Holly looked at the sleeping girl and was certain she didn't want to spend Christmas anywhere else. "I think that would be lovely. What do you think Becca would like for Christmas?"

"The Amish don't do gifts like the Englisch do. Our gifts are more often than not practical in nature and very basic. Wooden toys, a new doll that has been handmade, a new kitchen tool or something for the barn. What did you have in mind?"

Holly smiled. "A kitten? Mrs. Marlow said one of the delivery men in town mentioned their house cat recently had a litter of kittens. One of them is all black and has pure white mittens on its feet."

"That sounds like the picture she was coloring."

"I thought the same thing. Would it be okay with you if I got her the kitten?"

Evan reached across the buggy and touched her cheek gently. "I can't think of anything she would like more. Again, I must give you thanks."

"I just want to see her smile," Holly told him. "If it makes her happy and gives her something to smile about, it will be the best present I've ever received."

"I look forward to seeing smiles upon both of your faces then."

Holly slid Becca off of her lap and then smiled at Evan. "Don't get out. Thank you for today. Denke. I cannot tell you how much it meant to me to have the opportunity to meet my family."

"I can see it in your eyes. Gutennacht, Holly. But your thanks should be given to Gott, I was just an instrument to be used today. I will see you in a few days' time."

Holly slipped from the buggy and watched as he drove away. Instead of going straight into the house, she wandered around the side to where the porch swing hung. She sat down and then looked up at the sky. "God, I don't know if You remember me or not...it's been so long since I last talked to You. I just wanted to say thank You for letting me come here and for sending Evan to help me meet my grandparents. I am not at all sure what it is that is happening to me, but I really like being here. Around these people. Living this simple lifestyle. I can't imagine going back to the real world."

She paused for a moment and then added, "I can't

imagine never seeing Evan or Becca again. God, I've never been in love, and I'm not really sure this is even heading in that direction, but Evan is such a special person. So strong and dedicated to Becca and doing what is right, even if that means he has to put aside his own desires.

"When I hugged him, and then he hugged me back, I never wanted to leave his arms. It felt so safe there, something I haven't ever truly felt. I guess I was hoping I would find that security when I met my daed, but then I felt even more alone.

"I probably don't have any right to ask this, but could You please help me figure out what to do about these feelings I'm developing for Evan and Becca. I don't want to get my heart broken, and I don't want to see either of them hurt, but I'm falling for him. Show me which direction is right."

She finished her softly spoken prayer and looked up to see Mrs. Marlow standing on the patio. "That was a lovely prayer, dear. Be encouraged that God always hears our prayers. He might not answer in the way we would like, but He always hears us. Trust Him and everything will work out just fine."

Holly turned red, ashamed that someone else had heard her innermost thoughts. But as it was only Mrs. Marlow, she decided to brush it off as though it were nothing. She stood up. "I'm going to do my best. I met my grandparents and family today and they were so loving and welcoming… I can't wait to go back and visit again."

"I'm happy for you, Holly. Did you and Evan have a gut time as well?"

"We did, but Becca was quiet all day."

"She'll come around. She trusts you and that is a big step for her. Be patient, and she'll start talking again soon. You have to remember the horrors she witnessed. Children are resilient, she will bounce back, it'll just take a little time."

Holly nodded her head and then took a cleansing breath of the brisk air. "Evan said the storm was going to hit during the night."

Mrs. Marlow smiled. "There will be a fresh blanket of snow come morning. How about a cup of hot cocoa before you go to bed?"

"That sounds like just what I need." Holly followed her hostess into the kitchen. It was the perfect ending to a perfect day.

A Very Happy Christmas

Christmas morning...

Holly held the basket close to her chest, keeping the blanket Mrs. Marlow had loaned her over the top so that the bitter wind didn't chill what was inside. It was still fairly early, and she only hoped Becca wasn't yet out of bed and that she could be there when she came down the stairs.

Mr. Marlow had carted her over to Evan's house a few minutes earlier, promising to return in a few hours with Mrs. Marlow and the Christmas feast. Holly had thanked him kindly and headed for the back door.

Evan was sitting at the table sipping his first cup of coffee when she tapped gently on the window pane. He immediately opened the door and ushered her inside. "Happy Christmas! Becca just woke up and is getting dressed. You're just in time."

"Happy Christmas to you as well," she half thought about kissing him on the cheek just like she would have done at home if she passed on the greeting, but managed to stop herself. She took her mind away from his handsome face and back to the contents of her basket. "Good, I was hoping to get here before she came down for breakfast." A sound from inside the basket indicated the gift was becoming rather anxious.

"Sounds like someone is ready to get out," Evan chuckled softly. "Oh, here she comes now. The second stair from the bottom creaks."

Becca wandered into the kitchen, saw Holly, and froze. "Becca, come say hello to Holly. She came to see you on Christmas Day."

Becca looked between her uncle and Holly and then eyed the basket perched on the table. Her eyes widened when a plaintive mewling sound came from beneath the blanket. She edged towards the table and leaned against Holly's side. "Kitty?"

The whispered words were like angelic music to both adults' ears. Holly swallowed back tears and nodded. "Open it and find out." Becca climbed up onto the bench and carefully pulled back the blanket to reveal the black kitten with green eyes and white socks on all four feet. "Kitty!"

Becca gingerly lifted the kitten and cradled her to her neck, whispering to the animal which soon closed its eyes and purred loudly.

Holly felt tears spill over her cheeks and looked at Evan to see a similar response. "Do you like your gift, Becca?"

She smiled and nodded. "Uncle Evan, is he mine?"

Evan nodded and cleared his throat several times

before he could speak again. "Yes, Becca. The kitten is yours. Holly gave him to you."

Becca leaned over and gave Holly a big kiss on the cheek. "I love you, Holly."

Holly wrapped her arms around the little girl and the kitten and kissed the top of her head. "I love you too, sweetie. Merry Christmas."

Three months later...

"Holly, Uncle Evan is here," Becca called from the front porch of the Bontrager haus. Holly had returned to Philadelphia shortly after New Year's Day and within a week had no doubts whatsoever that she no longer belonged in the Englisch world. She missed the simplicity of reading by firelight or lantern. She missed the stillness of the evenings and the abundance of stars lighting up the ink-black sky when the bright lights of the city were not providing their unnatural glow.

She missed Evan and Becca. And they missed her.

On the day after Christmas, Evan had driven her to see her grandparents. A large dinner had been put together and for the next three days relatives arrived from near and far to make her acquaintance. Evan and Becca had only stayed for a few hours, and Evan had promised to return three days later to pick her up.

She loved getting to know her familye and after returning to Philadelphia, she'd realized she was too far away to see them very often. They didn't use telephones of course which left letter-writing their only means of communication. Without electricity, there were no computers or cell phones.

After going without a family for so long, she was loath to leave her newfound one so easily. She spoke it over with her editor, who agreed to her proposal of a freelance position to submit articles about the Amish lifestyle to the newspaper on a regular basis.

She'd discussed having to submit them in handwritten format, and he'd balked at first and then capitulated, provided her handwriting was legible. Holly had smiled and promised him her penmanship was excellent.

She didn't have much in the way of material items since her apartment was mostly furnished by local rent-to-own stores. They were more than happy to take their merchandise back, applying a substantial penalty, of course. She cancelled her credit cards, and sold her car. The whole process was liberating.

A week after returning to Philadelphia, she was more than ready to return to Old Repton. She'd spoken with Mrs. Marlow, who had offered her a room for as long as she wanted it. She planned to ask her grandparents about staying with them for a few weeks, and they'd been thrilled at the prospect of getting to know her better.

Three months later and she had finally come to a decision about the future direction of her life. She'd been learning all about the Amish faith and God and after talking with the bishop and her family at length, she'd decided to ask to be baptized into the Amish faith. It would not be a quick process, but it felt right. It felt for the first time as though she were coming home.

She enjoyed all there was to learn about the Amish way of life and religion. Most of all, she enjoyed the opportunity to spend time with her familye and new friends. Evan's farm was only a few miles away and he made the time to visit her at least once a week on the pretense of Becca and her spending time together.

Evan had brought Becca over today and then disappeared with one of Holly's uncles. Holly could tell he was planning something, but when he stepped into the haus and sent Becca outside for a moment, she knew without a doubt that her life was about to change.

"Holly, I know it's only been a few months, and I'm willing to wait a while if that is what you want, but I'm falling in love with you. Becca has loved you for a long time already. I wanted you to know that I wish to formally court you from this day forward, in the hopes that one day soon, maybe even this summer, you'll marry me." He paused. "If you are willing of course. I know it's soon and…"

Holly was stunned and elated. "Jah," she butted in "Of course I'll let you court me, and I'll even marry you when the time comes, but I want to be baptized into your faith first. It would only be right."

Evan grinned from ear to ear and then whispered, "This would be a good time to exercise your right to hug me. The bishop is nowhere to be seen and we're all alone."

Holly needed no further prodding and threw herself into his waiting arms. She hugged him tight and then closed her eyes. "Denke, Gott."

Evan squeezed in response to her whispered words.

"What are you thanking Gott for? Not that I'm not impressed about your use of the language of course. I'm just interested."

She laughed. Evan always had a way of turning a serious question into a comical one. "For you. For Becca. For bringing me here and letting me have this chance at happiness."

Evan hugged her tight and then set her away from him. "It is not necessary to tell most people, but I think in this instance your familye would appreciate hearing about our plans."

Holly nodded and held his hand as they stepped from the haus to find most of her familye gathered in the yard. "Did they know this was going to happen?"

Evan shrugged. "I might have said something the other night."

Holly grinned. "Well, no matter. I can't wait to tell Becca. I bet she wants to bring the cat to the ceremony."

Evan shook his head, laughing. "That is not going to happen. The cat stays at the haus."

Four months later...

Holly and Evan exchanged vows, becoming husband and wife in the eyes of Gott and their familye and friends. Becca stood slightly behind them holding a white wicker basket in both hands.

Holly had been correct in assuming that Becca would want to include the cat in the ceremony. Evan had tried to dissuade the little girl, trying to convince her that the cat would be a nuisance, but Becca had been insistent.

Holly had purchased the basket for her to use, and Evan had finally given up in the face of their united front.

Holly loved Becca as her own child, and she couldn't wait until Gott saw fit to bless her and Evan with children of their own. She was happier than she could ever remember and looked forward to the coming weeks when she and Evan would be travelling the country to visit with her relatives and his.

"Mrs. Miller, what are you smiling about?" Evan whispered next to her ear as she bid another group of guests farewell.

"Is there a reason I shouldn't be smiling?" she asked in response. "And I'm perfectly aware that we Amish don't use Mr. and Mrs. in conversations with ourselves, so you can drop the Mrs. Miller straight away, Evan."

He grinned as he ignored the fake rebuke. "Not that I can think of. Your aunt and uncle are taking Becca with them for the weekend. She seems to like their kinner well enough, and she even talks to them at times."

Becca still struggled with talking about certain things, but day by day and month by month Holly could tell it was becoming ever easier for the little girl.

"That is very nice of them," she said, knowing Becca's sleeping arrangements.

"Very. We've spoken with everyone and are more than okay to leave at any time."

Holly nodded and then looked around at the barn full of people who had come out to witness their marriage. "Let's go now, then."

Evan nodded and escorted her to the waiting buggy. Holly allowed him to hand her up into the buggy, and as word spread of their departure, everyone came out of the barn to wave them off. Contrasts amazed her and did so again now as she looked at the people who'd arrived to celebrate their marriage. She'd arrived in Old Repton an orphan, all alone in the world. She'd gained a new understanding of Gott, a familye, and a husband and dochder in the last eight months.

As they headed for Evan's farm, she placed a hand upon her stomach and ushered up a silent prayer to Gott to let there be a new addition to their little familye in ten months' time. A schweschder or bruder for Becca to play with, and a new little life to love and teach the ways of Gott to.

She reached for her new husband's hand and sighed contentedly. It had taken her a while to get to this point, but she was finally home and secure. She had just needed to find her roots. *Denke, Mamm for protecting me and I'm sorry if I hurt you. Gott, forgive me for my selfishness and help me never to forget where I've come from. Amen.*

Part Two

Finding a Family

One Year Later

Old Repton, Pennsylvania

Holly Miller, formerly Holly Sanders, was sitting on the front porch of the haus she shared with her husband and dochder. The kinner wasn't her biological child, but she loved her as if she were her very own. She was a beautiful child with a gentle spirit, an angelic singing voice, and the curiosity of the cat she so dearly loved.

Becca was currently playing with the cat in the yard and Evan was out working in the fields. Holly should have been writing her next installment for the newspaper in Philadelphia, but the numerous changes that had occurred over the last year had her procrastinating. So much had changed, and she had several topics in mind, she just couldn't seem to settle on only one.

Holly had come to Old Repton to find her mamm's familye after her untimely death and had gained not only an extensive familye network, but a husband and five-year-old little girl. She had abandoned the Englisch way of life and been baptized into the Amish faith a few weeks before marrying the man she'd fallen in love with, Evan Miller.

A year later she had no regrets. She loved the simplicity of her surroundings, the quiet time at the end of day which she spent with Evan and Becca, and the large familye she now had surrounding her. Grandparents, cousins, aunts and uncles, and an entire community of likeminded individuals she was growing to love and depend upon. She'd only been part of their lives for a short time, but they accepted her as if she'd been born here. It was the best feeling in the world and she'd never been so at peace with her life.

Her editor had allowed her to keep writing for the newspaper, although she now handwrote everything instead of typing it on a computer. She wrote a column every other week that provided fresh insights about the Amish way of life. Her column had been widely received by both the Amish and the Englischers. Her articles offered a brand-new approach to the subject, and her personal anecdotes were both delightful and informative, giving the readers a sense of being in an intimate relationship with the writer.

She loved her familye. Evan was such a kind and caring husband, and a beacon of light and faith to her from the very first. His niece, Becca, was the joy of Holly's life. Orphaned at the tender age of five when her parents were killed in a haus fire, Evan had taken her in and made her his own. She'd been so traumatized by the death of her parents that she had stopped talking completely. Until she met Holly.

Looking back on those early days, Holly still gave

Gott all the credit, even though she'd been the one Holly first spoke to. Becca had continued to improve while Holly tried to figure out the new course of her life. Since Evan and Holly's marriage, Becca had only improved more each day. Now when Becca was home and the haus became too quiet, Holly grew worried and went looking to see what new mischief the little girl was up to.

Holly smiled as she watched the little girl who'd stolen her heart play with the kitten. Becca had grown from a shy, quiet child into a lively and curious girl, interacting comfortably with the other children she came into contact with. And she loved to sing!

Holly paused in her recollections and listened. Becca was singing a song to the cat about a caterpillar they had discovered in the flower beds. She bit her lip so that her laughter wouldn't cause the little girl to stop.

"Caterpillar, caterpillar, fat and green," she sang in her little sing song voice, all the while trying to keep the cat from batting the caterpillar off the leaf it was curled up on. The scene was more than comical. Becca lifted the cat up around the middle, scolding it for trying to hurt their new friend as she carried him towards the haus.

Holly lost her battle not to laugh and chuckled softly to herself. Becca and the cat named Kitty went almost everywhere together. She'd tried to convince Evan and Holly that Kitty would be welcome at the Amish school, but Evan had shaken his head and declared that cats did not go to school. Holly had requested that Kitty stay at home to keep her company. Her request had gone over much better than Evan's declaration, and both accomplished the same thing in the end.

Becca looked at her. "Holly, why are you laughing?"

"What is that song you're singing?" she asked in reply, making her way down the porch steps to see the caterpillar for herself.

Becca smiled. "Kitty found a caterpillar." She set the cat down on the porch with a shake of her finger and a stern demand that the animal stay put and then turned and followed at Holly's heels.

Holly observed the small creature for a moment with a smile. Becca loved to sing and did so all about the house. That didn't bother Holly in the least because the little girl had a beautiful voice. Becca had even been convinced to join the school choir, despite her young age. At only six years old she was finally out of her shell and Evan and Holly were doing all they could to get her involved and keep her talking.

"That's a lovely caterpillar. It will one day turn into an even prettier butterfly." Holly wasn't sure what kind of butterfly and was thankful that Becca didn't ask. "Would you and Kitty like to help me prepare dinner?" she asked, standing up and turning back towards the haus.

Becca nodded and lifted the cat when she was on the top step of the porch. "Can we have a snack?"

Holly smiled. "You may have a snack and Kitty may have a bowl of milk."

"Yay!" Becca hurried towards the haus, the kitten allowing himself to be carried around by the little arms that grasped him around his middle. Holly looked after them, feeling blessed to have them both in her life. Moving to Old Repton and becoming Amish had been the greatest blessing in her life.

The Visitor

Several weeks later...

Summertime was fully underway in Old Repton and with the warmer temperatures came the multitude of tourists. Some came to gawk at the Amish and their strange clothing and customs, but mostly they were there to shop and escape the hustle and bustle of the cities and spend a day or two ensconced in the simple life. But it was only a novelty for most and at the end of their visit they would return to their busy lives, electronic devices, and modern technology.

As a way to help educate the tourists, daily tours were offered around the Amish countryside in horse-drawn buggies, which provided the opportunity to see the Amish farms and shops up close and personal. The younger menner of the Community drove the buggies, collected the fares, and provided detailed explanations about each farm visited. Many Amish had declared that they were too busy to interact with the tourists in such a fashion, but for the most part everyone was pleasant and tried their best to be polite and courteous while they were being observed like bugs beneath a microscope.

Having grown up in the Englisch world, it was much easier for Holly to understand the Englisch fascination with the Amish lifestyle. They all dressed alike, were modest in all things, and eschewed modern technologies. A complete one hundred and eighty degrees from the way in which most Englisch lived, including Holly in the years before she embarked on her quest and found her Amish familye.

Holly and Evan continued to take their fruits and vegetables to the farmer's market in town, and it seemed that everyone loved to buy the fresh produce that Evan labored to grow. Holly helped him by manning the tables, and she had no trouble smiling and conversing with those who knew nothing about the Amish lifestyle.

Holly did her best to answer their questions, having learned much about the Amish culture during her year of marriage to Evan. She remembered her fascination with their culture in those early days, and also the misconceptions that seemed to exist in the Englisch world. She tried to educate the tourists to the best of her ability and understanding, and always did so with a smile in place.

Her time amongst the Amish hadn't been all smiles and flowers, though. A couple of months back, Holly had suffered a miscarriage, losing her first child when she wasn't yet halfway through her pregnancy. She and Evan had been quite ecstatic when they learned about the pregnancy so soon after their marriage. Holly had taken it as a sign that Gott was blessing their union and her decision to become Amish. But then tragedy had struck.

Four months into her pregnancy, the contractions had set in which necessitated a trip to the doctor. Unfortunately, there was nothing to be done and she miscarried the boppli; even though Evan had tried his best to be there for her, the days and weeks following the loss of their first boppli had left Holly filled with sorrow and a deep depression. She'd grieved the loss of their first kinner and the more she'd tried to pretend for those around her, the worse her depression became. Only by the grace of Gott and Evan's steadfast love and understanding, did she finally start to return to her normal, happy self. Those were dark days, some of the darkest she'd ever faced which, given the losses she'd already suffered in her life, was hard to fathom. She'd grieved the loss of the daed she'd never known, and the death of her mamm, but losing her first boppli was tantamount to having a knife slashed through her very soul.

She spent many days questioning Gott and trying to accept what had happened. Had it not been for Bishop Miller and his wise counsel, she wasn't sure she would have been able to let go of the guilt she felt. There was no right or wrong way to feel after losing a baby. As time moved on immediately after the miscarriage, Holly suffered through grief, guilt, emptiness, fear, and loneliness. She mourned the boppli she had loved but never held. Did she cause her baby's death through something she did or did not do during the pregnancy? She would wake up with an emptiness in her belly which crept like spilled water through her body and soaked her very soul, and then the loneliness overcame her. A loneliness suffered despite being surrounded by the people she loved; the ones who supported her through it all. The doctor at the hospital had told both Holly and Evan that the miscarriage had been a freak occurrence and that she had no blame in losing the boppli. As the days and weeks passed, she came to realize the truth of that fact, and she knew that without the love and support of Evan and her familye she might not have pulled herself together. Evan was such a hardworking mann, and he labored tirelessly on the farm to provide for them all. His steadfastness had helped pull her out of her depression and she was determined to face each day as it came and do whatever she could to be a good helpmate to her husband.

Holly helped out wherever she could, selling their milk and produce at the farmer's market in town, taking care of the household chores, and doing all she could to carry the load around the farm. She also contributed the money she earned through her writing to help pay for the familye's expenses. This made her happy and she knew Evan was appreciative of the ease with which she had taken to the Amish way of life.

One afternoon, Holly was at home tending to the daily chores when a knock came on the front door. She dried her hands and opened the door to see a young woman standing on the doorstep. "Gutentag. Can I help you?"

The young woman looked at her and then stated quickly, "I'm Megan Sanders."

Holly repeated the name inside her head, alarm bells going off in her brain. *Sanders? As in Brian Sanders, my father?* "What can I do for you?" she asked, not wanting to borrow trouble if it wasn't already there. She knew that there were many people with the last name of Sanders in this world.

"You are Holly Sanders, right?" the young woman asked nervously, wringing her hands together.

Holly shook her head. "Nee, I'm Holly Miller now. I got married last year."

The young woman nodded her head and then rushed to get out what she had come to say, as if afraid she might chicken out before she had done so. "I'm your sister, well…your half-sister."

Schweschder? Holly swallowed back the dismay that wanted to spew forth and remembered her manners. "Would you like to come in?"

The young woman looked unsure for a moment and then gingerly stepped inside the haus. She was very hesitant and looked somewhat lost as she followed Holly into the kitchen and took a seat at the kitchen island. Once seated she seemed to be stumped as to where to begin her explanation. Holly took pity on her and tried to help her along.

"Megan, why are you here?" She gave her what she hoped was a smile of encouragement, doing her best to hide the questions zipping through her brain.

"I wanted to get to know you."

Holly smiled at her encouragingly. "And how did you know where to find me?"

"I was going through some of my father's stuff…

er, well, I guess I should say…our father's stuff and found a photo of you when you were only a baby. Your name was on the back and then I found a shoebox full of newspaper clippings. You're a journalist?"

Holly nodded, amazed to hear that her daed had known anything about her. She was even more shocked to hear that he'd kept track of her all these years and wasn't quite sure what to make of that information. She'd thought her daed had all but forgotten her, and now to find out that he'd been following her career…it brought tears to her eyes to know that he hadn't completely abandoned her.

Holly pulled herself together and looked at the young woman who claimed to be her younger schweschder. "Megan, tell me about your life."

Megan did so, and Holly spent the afternoon learning about the young woman's life thus far. She learned that her schweschder wasn't only looking to build a relationship with Holly, she was in fact attempting to run away from her problems. Holly hoped she could be of some help in that regard.

As the day wore on, she became cognizant of the fact that Megan really had nowhere else to go. Holly saw Evan returning from the fields and go into the barn. "Megan, will you excuse me for a moment?"

When Megan nodded, Holly hurried out to the barn, greeting Becca and Evan when she stepped inside. "Evan. Becca. We have company."

Evan looked up from where he was tending to the tack and Becca came running to greet her. "Holly!"

Holly swung the little girl up into her arms and

hugged her close for a moment and then set her back down. "I need to speak with your uncle for a moment."

Becca wasn't sure she liked being dismissed, but when Holly simply held her gaze and then nodded towards the barn doors, Becca sighed and went in search of her cat, leaving Holly alone with Evan.

"What's up? Who's come to visit? I saw the vehicle parked in the driveway," Evan asked, hanging the bridle he held in his hands up on the wall.

Holly smiled at him. "My schweschder."

Evan looked at her curiously. "I didn't know you had any siblings?"

Holly shook her head. "Neither did I until a few hours ago. It seems my daed remarried and had another boppli besides me."

Evan came to her side and looked down into her eyes. "This is gut?"

Holly nodded slowly. "I think so. She seems so lost. I would like to ask her to stay with us for a day or two…"

Evan wrapped an arm around her shoulders and turned her towards the barn doors. "She is familye. She is welcome to stay as long as she likes. Come, introduce me to this new schweschder and then I will wash up for dinner."

A Silent Prayer

Two days later...

Megan had readily accepted Holly and Evan's invitation to stay with them, although she was quite clearly not prepared for the simple life they lived. The absence of electricity hadn't seemed to register with her until the sun went down on her first night in their haus. The use of the oil lanterns and candles had caused a look of surprise and mild terror. Holly had laughed and showed her how to light and extinguish the lanterns before showing her to their guest bedroom.

This was now day two and Holly was pleased to see Megan starting to settle in a bit. She'd learned much about her schweschder over the last few days, including the fact that she was a college student at the University of Philadelphia and that she had suffered with depression for years. Considering Holly had just come through a dark time herself, she had great empathy for the young woman.

She'd also discovered that their daed's passing had exacerbated Megan's depression. She'd not been on good terms with her mother, which had only served to make the loss that much harder to deal with. Holly suspected that her problems with her mamm were what had really sent her in search of her schweschder, but she couldn't prove that. Yet.

They now sat on the porch watching Becca play with her cat, and Holly listened to Megan speak about a mann she'd personally never had the opportunity to know. Their daed.

"He really was a good man," Megan told her. "He met my mother when they were both fairly young."

"They got married because they were in love?" Holly asked.

Megan shook her head. "No. They got married because my mother fell pregnant with me, but that isn't to say they weren't in love. They were. Brian was a recovering alcoholic and when I got a little bit older, I realized that each day was a struggle for him to stay dry."

Holly was confused and asked, "I thought he was living in a homeless shelter when he died?"

Megan nodded sadly. "There was a time when he attended the AA meetings religiously, he even became a mentor to new alcoholics for a short while, but his determination withered over the years. He relapsed and started drinking again, and things went from bad to worse. I remember so many fun times with him when I was younger…" She met Holly's eyes. "He really was a good man, he just had a terrible illness."

Holly laid a comforting hand on Megan's arm for a

moment and then she withdrew it. "Tell me about your mamm." When Megan looked confused at the Amish term, Holly smiled. "Your mother. Tell me about your mother."

"What was the word you used instead?" Megan asked.

"Mamm. It is the Amish word for mother."

"Mamm… I like the way that sounds," Megan told her with a smile. "My mamm is a psychologist and a professor at the University."

"She works long hours?" Holly asked.

Megan nodded. "She often has to stay on campus well into the evening for meetings or University events…she wasn't home a lot."

Holly began to better understand Megan's childhood years. "So, while she was at work, you helped take care of daed?"

Megan smiled. "Yes." She frowned and looked down at her hands which were constantly worrying the fringe on her T-shirt. "At least, until I was twelve."

"What happened when you were twelve?" Holly asked.

"They got a divorce. He was drinking all the time then and whenever she was home they fought horribly. She kicked him out of the house."

"And he went to the local homeless shelter," Holly surmised, having discovered that fact while looking for her father a year earlier.

Megan nodded. "Yes. She gave up too quickly on him. If she'd just tried a little harder, he could have found the help he needed…" She broke off on a sob and

Holly realized that their daed's death had been devastating for the young girl. Megan was even more distressed than Holly had been when she discovered their father's obituary in the local newspaper. That seemed like a different world and a very long time ago to her now.

"Did you and your mamm work things out? After his death?" Holly asked, seeing so many similarities between herself and this young girl.

Megan shook her head. "I haven't spoken to her since then."

Holly raised a brow. "Not at all?"

Megan shook her head. "Not really. She washed her hands of our father and has moved on."

Holly wasn't sure she understood. "Moved on?"

Megan nodded. "She's getting married again. In fact, she should have already tied the knot with her new husband. The wedding was last week, I think." She sneered at the words and Holly said nothing. It was obvious that Megan wasn't in agreement with her mamm's decision to remarry. Having never met the woman, Holly didn't feel qualified to offer any opinion on the matter.

Instead, she let silence rule the moment as they sat on the porch, rocking in the wooden chairs crafted by someone in the Community. Holly took the opportunity to offer up a silent prayer for wisdom and guidance where Megan was concerned.

Gott, please give me the words to help her heal. It is not right for a dochder and mamm to be at odds with one another. If there is a way for their relationship to heal, please make it visible. Your will be done.

New Life

A few days later...

The more Holly learned about her schweschder and her daed, the more she had to deal with feelings of envy and jealousy. She was happy that Megan had such good memories of their daed and that he'd been able to taste sobriety for a while after Megan's birth, but at the same time she envied Megan. The young woman had been given a chance to know the man they both called father, while Holly had been denied that chance.

But those feelings were negative, and Holly had learned this past year to focus on the good things in life, so she pushed them aside and turned her attention to helping Megan with her problems. She listened politely as Megan shared her life story, how she searched for their daed and found him living in the homeless shelter and then confronted her mamm.

"She really didn't care," Megan told Holly as they worked side-by-side in the garden. Megan hadn't had a clue how to work in the fresh dirt, but she was an avid learner and while her hands were kept busy she was able to tell her side of the story without the emotions bogging her down. She'd been so melancholic; Holly and Evan had discussed whether or not she was in need of medical intervention for her depression. They'd been unaware that she'd already been given help, she just wasn't sure if she wanted to continue with it.

"Are you so sure of that?" Holly asked, placing a ripe tomato in the basket near her feet. "I'm sure she must have cared a little bit."

"If she did, she hid it well. She didn't even want his things in the house. She boxed them all up and tossed them in the trash pile. I rescued them and stored them in the garage, hoping he would come back one day."

"And that's where you found my picture?" Holly guessed.

Megan nodded. "After I found out he'd died, I spent several days going through those boxes and his desk. She hadn't wanted anything of his in the house and had turned his office into a sitting room. She got rid of all the furniture and stored it in the garage."

"Did she know you had kept the boxes of his things?" Holly wanted to know.

Megan shrugged. "I don't know if she knew at the onset, but she figured it out when I confronted her with your photo. She refused to answer me, so I researched you myself. That's how I ended up here. I contacted the newspaper you write for and finally got in touch with your editor. After telling him my story, he told me I should look for you here."

Holly made a mental note to thank her editor with her next submission. She knew that he had to have been very moved by Megan's story to break his own rule against sharing personal information about his employees. Under the circumstances, she was thankful he could bend his own rules from time to time.

Holly smiled at her schweschder. "I'm glad you sought me out." Holly could see that Megan was a bright girl with a very kind heart. Even though Megan seemed very melancholic now, Holly could understand where that came from. Their stories were very similar, and she only hoped that their outcomes wouldn't be the same.

Holly had once been estranged from her own mamm, but before she could mend those fences, her mamm had died and Holly had been left alone, without the benefit of being able to apologize and take back the hateful words she'd spoken. She still had to deal with daily feelings of regret, and if she could do anything to help fix things for Megan, she was willing to do so. She would give anything for a chance to apologize to her mamm, or to take back the hateful words they'd last exchanged. That opportunity was lost to her, but not to Megan. Hope remained for these two to mend what was broken between them.

"Megan, I know things with your mamm are strained, but have you thought about trying to contact her and having an adult conversation with her?"

Megan shook her head. "All we do is fight. It's no use."

"I understand that, more than you probably realize." Holly shared with Megan the details of her relationship with her own mamm and then she advised her, "I wish you would consider abandoning your pride and make the choice to try again with your mamm. Believe me, things can change quickly, and I would hate for you to lose that chance because your pride was more important to you than mending fences with her."

Holly thought she might have said too much, but rather than being upset, Megan nodded her head and appeared to at least be considering her words. She could see how turbulent Megan's feelings were. Coupled with her youth, Holly wondered what she could say that might make a difference. Not willing to give up, and having already spoken to Evan about this matter, she met her schweschder's gaze. "Would you like to stay with us for another week?"

Megan looked at her. "Really? You and Evan wouldn't mind?"

Holly smiled at her. "We would love to have you here. Tomorrow is the farmer's market and you could go with me and meet some of the people who live here. Would you like that?"

Megan placed the squash she held in her hands inside the packing box by her side and then looked up with a nod. "Yes, I would love to stay here a while longer." She grinned. "I kind of thought you all were crazy, living without electricity and telephones and such, but the peace and quiet is kind of growing on me."

When Holly opened her mouth to speak, Megan shook her head and held up a hand. "Not that I'm wanting to live here permanently, mind you. But it's been a nice little break from everything. You know?"

Holly chuckled and picked up the basket of tomatoes.

"Jah, I know. But unlike you, I chose not to return to that crazy, hectic world of cell phones and schedules, and constantly feeling like there's too much to do and not enough hours in a day to accomplish it all. I love my new life here, and I look forward to showing you around over the next few days."

Trust

One week later...

The week flew by and Holly and Becca loved having Megan staying over with them. Evan spent more time than ever in the fields and taking care of the farm animals, but each evening he returned to the haus and listened to the women talking. He was pleased to observe the bond that was quickly forming between the two women. He thanked Gott for sending Megan to Holly, believing that the timing of her arrival had been perfect to help Holly to move forward and leave her sorrow behind.

Megan seemed to be enjoying her time with them and he was surprised to see how enthusiastically she had taken to certain aspects of the Amish lifestyle. At the age of twenty-seven, there were often occasions for him to pinch himself to accept that Holly was truly his wife. He was so happy that she'd adapted to living the

Amish lifestyle and, despite the many changes she'd undergone in the last year, she never complained.

He worked hard each day to make their farm prosperous, and Holly had proven to be a very capable and energetic helper. She adored Becca, and his niece returned the sentiment more than wholeheartedly.

"Becca's asleep," Holly whispered as she joined him once more in the living room.

He looked up from staring at his Bible where he had been lost in his thoughts and smiled at her. He held a hand out to her and she joined him, gingerly sitting on his lap as he closed the Bible and set it on the side table. "Did you and Megan have a gut day?"

Holly settled back against his chest, closing her eyes and savoring these few moments alone with her husband. Becca was asleep, and Megan had retired to the guest bedroom located just off the kitchen. She and Evan would retire upstairs to their room in a few moments, but right now he just wanted to enjoy holding her in his arms. Safe and very much loved.

Holly sighed. "We sold almost all the produce at the farmer's market today."

"That is unusual," Evan remarked, normally they had enough to last both days. "What was different?"

"A buyer for an Englisch restaurant purchased most everything and said he would be back again next week. I promised him we would bring more next week."

Evan kissed her on the forehead. "We will indeed. How did Megan like meeting our friends and neighbors?"

"She seems to be adjusting well, but I'm not sure

that is a gut thing. She is only nineteen…so young and with so much of her life before her. She is on summer break right now, but her classes at the University will start again in the Fall."

"Has she said anything more about her mamm?" he asked, knowing that the rift betwcen them weighed heavily on Holly's mind.

"Not so far. I'm hoping to speak with her about the issue of calling Linda again."

"Gott will guide you, trust Him." He hugged her and then set her off his lap and rose from the chair. "I'll check the locks."

Holly smiled at him and blew out all but one of the lanterns. Evan came back and took her hand to walk up the stairs with her by his side. Her miscarriage earlier in the year had put a lot of strain on their marriage, but they had managed to pull through that dark time and their relationship was stronger than ever for it. Suffering a miscarriage can have a profound effect on a couple's relationship. The shared loss can either tear them apart or bring them closer together. That all depends on how they handle it. Evan understood that their unborn bop-pli was probably more real to Holly than to him. She experienced the baby physically, and her body changed to become a mother. The doctors had explained to Evan that while many fathers only feel the baby has become real after they get to hold it once it is born, mothers bond with their unborn during the pregnancy. What brought Evan and Holly closer after the devastation of losing their boppli was the fact that they wholeheartedly supported one another through it all every step of the way.

They did not resort to blame and guilting one another but loved one another through the loss and the pain.

Evan loved being a father to Becca, but he truly wanted more kinner, as did Holly. He knew Holly's mind had been preoccupied with trying to help her schweschder, but that didn't mean he couldn't also get her thinking about their future. He wasn't sure how things would work out for Megan, but he was sure that Holly and he had a bright future ahead and, with Gott's blessings, that future would include kinner of their own.

Holly walked with Evan to their bedroom, pushing aside her concerns over Megan. She'd spent most of the last week focusing on Megan and the silence between her and her mamm. This time, right now, was for her and her husband.

She recalled how special the end of each day had been when she and Evan were first married. The haus was quiet and the chores were all done until the next sunrise, Becca was sleeping peacefully in her own bed, and it was just the two of them.

Evan had been so patient with her through the last few months and, as she opened their bedroom door and stepped inside, she looked forward to moving forward with building their familye. She didn't know what Gott had in store for them, but she trusted Him to have their best interests at heart and to give them exactly what they needed, when they were ready to receive it. Faith. It was something she'd learned more about since becoming Amish and it had fast become the driving force behind each new day.

Unwelcome Interruption

~❧~

Two days later...

Megan, Becca, and Holly were just finishing up the bread they'd started making earlier that morning when a knock came upon the front door.

"I'll get it," Becca yelled out, climbing down from the chair on which she had been standing.

Holly shook her head and halted the little girl before she could take a second step. "Nee. You need to go wash the flour off your hands and face first. I will see who has come to visit." Holly accompanied her words with a smile and Becca nodded in compliance.

Holly walked to the front door and opened it to see an unfamiliar woman standing there with a significant frown on her face. "Gutentag. Can I help you?" Holly asked softly.

The woman looked her up and down, obviously finding fault with Holly's appearance. "I'm here to get my daughter."

Holly took a step back at the vehemence in the woman's tone and struggled for words. After a short pause, she swallowed. "You must be Linda?" Holly stepped forward and extended her hand to the woman, who ignored it and tried to see past her into the haus.

"Where is my daughter?!" the woman raised her voice. "Megan! Megan, you get out here right now!"

Holly turned when she heard feet enter the room behind her. "Mother? What are you doing here?" Megan asked incredulously.

Holly stepped to the side and watched as Linda took in her dochder's attire. Megan had commented several times on the simple dresses of the Amish women, driving Holly to alter one of her own dresses to fit the young woman so that she would blend better at the farmer's market.

"I'm here to get you out of here." Linda turned back to Holly. "How dare you keep my daughter here, filling her head with all manner of ideas and brainwashing her..."

Holly shook her head in denial. "Linda, we have done nothing but befriend Megan and allow her to stay with us. Please, won't you come inside?"

Linda gave Holly a derisive glance and then stalked into the haus, glowering at what she saw. "I can't believe you've been hiding out...here!"

Megan gave Holly a scared look, her face red with embarrassment. "How did you find me?"

Linda shook her head. "That doesn't really matter. You need to come with me."

"I don't want to."

"You're nineteen, you don't know what's good for you."

"I'm an adult and I can make my own decisions,"

Megan retorted. "You've got your new husband! Go away and leave me alone!"

"Megan, stop acting childish!"

Holly could see that matters were spiraling out of control quickly and she stepped forward. "Linda, would you like something to drink? Maybe a cup of tea, or..."

Linda rounded on her. "No! I don't want anything to eat or drink. I want you to stop brainwashing my daughter and making her hate me."

"Mamm!" Megan called out, using the Amish term without thinking about it.

"What did you just call me?" Linda asked in a deceptively calm voice.

Holly gave her a small smile. "She called you 'mother', she just used the Amish term."

"See, brainwashing. Get your things, you're leaving with me."

Megan crossed her arms over her chest. "Nee! I won't go. In case you're wondering, that's the Amish equivalent for No!"

Linda looked between Holly and Megan and then made a harsh noise. "You're just like your worthless father. I don't know why I even bothered." She turned, pushed Holly aside, and stormed from the haus, almost knocking Becca over in her haste to leave.

Holly watched her go, her heart breaking for the devastation on both women's faces. They needed to find common ground and remember that they loved one another, and soon!

"I'm so sorry..." Megan began once Becca was settled in the kitchen with her cat and a snack.

"What are you apologizing for?" Holly asked her softly.

"My mother…"

"Don't apologize for the actions of another," Holly advised her.

"But I dragged this mess to your front door. My mother's words and actions…"

"…are based on the love she has for you. And I don't see what just happened as a mess, just a matter of miscommunication. I'm sure your mamm is incredibly worried about you and just doesn't know how to convey that to you right now."

"She has a funny way of showing she cares," Megan muttered.

"Maybe, but she's only human and as such, not perfect." She paused for a moment and then asked, "If you were in her position, and your only kinner had taken off and you'd not known where she was or when she might be coming home, wouldn't you be terribly worried about her safety and wellbeing?"

Megan looked at Holly, and after a time she reluctantly nodded her head. "I guess?"

Holly nodded and smiled at her answer. "Of course you would. Is it so crazy to think that your mamm harbors the same feelings towards you?"

"Still, she shouldn't have acted as if you did something wrong," Megan continued.

Holly waved her concerns away. "It really is okay. Schweschders should look after one another and so should mamms. Everything she said comes from a place of unrivalled love in her heart. If nothing else, believe that."

Harm's Way

~

Later that same night...

Megan waited until everyone in the haus was fast asleep before she quietly snuck out through the back door off the kitchen. Since her mamm's visit earlier that day, she'd been in a state of embarrassment and turmoil. Her mother's actions had been completely over the top as far as she was concerned, and yet Holly had been so kind and understanding.

Evan had been sympathetic and had even prayed with her before heading off to bed. Megan wasn't sure what to do next. She'd come here seeking information from her schweschder and looking for some sort of respite from her thoughts. Depression had plagued her for years and had become even more pressing on her thoughts since discovering her daed's death.

She smiled to herself in the dark as she automatically substituted the Amish terms for her parents. A loud crack of thunder overhead had her jumping in her shoes and hurrying towards her vehicle. Since her arrival in Old Repton, the car had remained parked beneath a large oak tree to the side of the horse barn. She'd not really wanted to drive it, and yet tonight, amidst the heavy storm clouds that were threatening to release a torrent of rain on the landscape, she wanted to be nowhere else. *I'll just leave my problems here. If no one can find me, then my problems won't be able to either.*

She slid behind the steering wheel and turned the key, relieved when the engine rumbled to life. She turned on the lights and another loud crack of thunder and lightning lit up the sky, making the silhouette of the surrounding structures seem ominous and dangerous in her eyes.

She backed up carefully and then headed the vehicle down the dirt lane that led to the paved country road. It was raining in earnest now and as she turned the windshield wipers on, she was reminded that the driver's side was broken and was only able to clear the bottom portion of the window.

Megan squinted into the night, struggling to find the yellow center line in the road between the flashes of lightning and the rain coming down in large windswept sheets. She felt her tires find the pavement and she headed to her right, not really knowing or caring where she was headed. I need to get away from here. Everything was ruined now because of her!

She wasn't in her right state of mind, she simply wanted to get away from her life. Away from the mother who wanted to control her life and tell her how she should feel. She used the Englisch term now, her anger at her mother making it easy to forego using the Amish term Megan considered much more intimate. She began to cry, and her emotions swelled, overwhelming her thoughts and making coherent thought almost impossible.

She felt the tires slip on the wet surface of the road, but rather than slowing down, she pressed the gas pedal harder. Since coming to Old Repton, she'd not been taking her anti-depressant medication and the emotions of the day were proving to be more than she could adequately handle on her own.

Her doctor had warned her never to miss a dose of the anti-depressants she was prescribed. He had made no bones about the severity of the side effects that would befall her if she did not take the medication every day at the same time. Megan was now well into experiencing many of the symptoms he had warned her about. It had started with heightened feelings of annoyance and irritability which had escalated rapidly to constant anxiety. Not only her mind was affected though. She felt as if a fuzzy television screen was running through her blood. Her touch, smell, and sight became increasingly sensitive to the point that the rain and lightning now even seemed to be coursing through her. It was not just a fuzzy head but a fuzzy body in its entirety. She fluctuated between the sensation of trying to run through water. Where every effort was futile, and she just exhausted herself even trying to accomplish even the most menial task. Then the sensation of being underwater would unexpectedly take hold and it was as if all around her became unclear. She would be aware of people communicating and interacting with her, but she would be unable to understand their words or connect with them on any level. Disassociated. Bewildered. Anxious. Paranoid. Confused.

Her eyes were filled with tears when the car hit another patch of water and skidded out of control, heading towards the side of the road with alarming speed. She righted the vehicle and kept driving. When the road ended, she turned right again, pushing on the gas pedal to speed down another dark country road. The lights of a small town blinked in the distance, but Megan wasn't concerned with reaching them. She just wanted to be left alone.

She'd been driving for a good thirty minutes in the pouring rain, and her shoulders were tight with the stress of trying to see the road ahead. She'd hydroplaned several times and managed to keep the car on the road; in another frame of mind she would have pulled over, realizing the roads were too unsafe to drive. But she was lost inside a depression so deep she could see nothing ahead of her but the need to get further away from where she thought she'd left her problems.

A flash of lightning illuminated the road ahead and she screamed as a large tree branch fell right in front of her car. She slammed her foot on the brake, but the water on the road prevented the tires from gripping the asphalt and her car careened off the road, coming to a stop only when the front end collided with a large tree. Megan's head slammed forward, hitting the steering wheel, and as her body recoiled and slid to the side, she felt a single sharp stab of pain and then everything went blessedly black.

A few moments later, a passerby saw the headlights of a vehicle, their beams shining through the pouring rain and telling the story of an unfortunate driver this night. The stranger used his cell phone to contact the local emergency dispatcher and then waited nearby until the ambulance arrived some five minutes later.

He could see the crumpled body inside the mangled vehicle, but given the weather conditions, he hadn't tried to open the door for fear of causing the occupant more injury. After giving his statement to the policeman who arrived a few moments later, he was assured they were doing everything they could for the young woman in the car and there was nothing for him to do.

He offered up a silent prayer for the nameless young woman and headed home to his wife and children, thankful they were all safe and out of harm's way this night.

Bad News

The next morning...

Holly was in the barn milking the cows when she heard the unmistakable sound of tires on the driveway. She put down the pail of warm milk and took up position in the doorway of the barn, looking towards the haus as Evan came out on the porch with a still sleepy Becca in his arms. She hadn't seen Megan yet this day but given the emotions of the day before she wasn't surprised the young woman was still asleep in her bed.

Holly walked towards the black police car as it came to a stop and a uniformed man stepped out, greeting Evan by name and with a somber shake of their hands.

"Gutentag, Officer Daniels. What brings you out this fine morning?" Evan asked. The rain the night before had washed away the dust clinging to the air and the sun had risen to greet a brilliant blue sky with nary a cloud in sight.

"Evan, I come with some bad news I'm afraid."

Holly came to stand besides her husband and watched the officer carefully, taking Becca from his arms and cuddling her against her shoulder. "Bad news?"

The officer nodded his head. "We wouldn't have known where to go except the Muellers were at the hospital getting ready to deliver their fourth baby when the ambulance arrived."

Evan placed an arm around Holly's shoulders and asked, "Ambulance?"

"There was an accident out on the highway sometime early this morning. A young woman by the name of Megan Sanders was driving."

Holly gasped and turned towards the haus. Megan's still asleep, isn't she? She looked back at Evan and he held on to her arm, holding her place.

"Are you sure it was Megan Sanders?" he asked, taking Becca back so that Holly didn't drop the little girl.

Officer Daniels nodded. "Afraid so. She ran into a tree during last night's storm and was out cold when they brought her in."

"Is she alright?" Evan asked, seeing that Holly seemed to have lost her voice.

"She hasn't woken up yet, but my information's a little old. She's at the hospital in town and I believe they've also contacted her mother, Linda Sanders, who is on her way."

Holly held on to her emotions until the officer left and then she turned to Evan with a stricken look upon her face. "What was she doing out on the highway in last night's storm?"

Evan shook his head and led her back into the haus.

"Help Becca get dressed and I'll finish up in the barn. After breakfast, we'll drive to the hospital and you can see her for yourself."

Holly nodded her head and took Becca out of his arms. "Come on, sweetie. We'll get you some breakfast as well."

"What's wrong with Megan?" the little girl asked, rubbing sleep from her eyes.

"She crashed her automobile." Holly looked to the side of the horse barn and was amazed that she hadn't noticed the vehicle missing this morning when she'd been about her chores. She had known how upset Megan had been last night, but she'd seemed much calmer after Evan had prayed with her. Had she taken off in her car because she was so upset with her mamm?

She helped Becca wash and get dressed, silently praying for Gott to intervene in this situation and fix whatever was wrong with Megan. She also offered up a prayer for wisdom and guidance should she encounter Linda at the hospital. After the heated exchange of the day before, Holly didn't want to be the cause of any more discord between mamm and dochder.

She fixed a hasty breakfast of fried eggs and buttered bread before Evan loaded them up into the buggy and they set off for the hospital. It wasn't a very large facility and Holly felt somewhat relieved that they hadn't transferred Megan to the big city hospital. That had to mean she wasn't seriously injured, right?

Understanding

They arrived at the hospital late in the morning and Holly inquired at the information desk for Megan's room number.

"She's on the third floor, room three twenty-eight. If you could please sign in here, you can head on up."

Holly signed her name and then started to add Evan's, but he stopped her. She looked up at him questioningly.

He shook his head. "I'm going to take Becca over to the duck pond while you go visit your schweschder. We'll come up a bit later."

Holly nodded and kissed Becca on the forehead. "Be gut."

"I will. Kiss Megan's owie and make it all better."

Holly gave the little girl a smile, wishing it could be that simple. However, she had a hunch that what troubled Megan couldn't be cured quite as easily. Whatever it was that had sent her out into the storm had to be a hurt that ran soul deep. Bumps and bruises would heal quickly compared to the depression and troubled soul Holly had glimpsed in her schweschder.

She took the stairs, using the extra time to pray for guidance and healing. She found the right room easily enough and pushed the slightly ajar door open to find Megan in the bed. She sported a black eye, a large bruise on her forehead, and her left arm was set in a cast.

Linda sat next to the bed, her forehead resting on the mattress. Her eyes were closed as she slept. Holly tried to be as quiet as a mouse, but her shoes squeaked on the tiled flooring and Linda blinked her eyes open and lifted her head. She gave Holly a somber glance and then pointed towards the opposite chair in a simple invitation. "Please?" she whispered.

Holly took a seat on the opposite side of the bed and then smoothed a tender hand over her schweschder's forehead, being careful not to apply any pressure on the large bruise. "Has she woken up yet?"

Linda shook her head sadly, tears in her eyes. "No. Not once since she arrived. The doctors say there is nothing to worry about, but then they aren't her mother."

Holly reached over and laid a comforting hand on Linda's before withdrawing it, hoping not to have crossed a boundary best left in place. Linda took a deep breath and then met her eyes. "I'm sorry for the way I behaved yesterday. I was rude, and it was unacceptable. I hope you can forgive me."

Holly gave her a smile. "Apology accepted, although it is not necessary. You were worried about your dochder, I completely understand."

Linda looked at her for a moment and then nodded. "I believe you do." She looked back at Megan. "She's been so upset with me for so many years. Ever since her father and I divorced, things have been strained between us. She seems to think there was more I could have done to make him quit drinking, but there wasn't. I tried everything and finally came to the conclusion that he had to want to quit for himself. Not for me and not for her. For him. He just couldn't do it."

Holly nodded. "I blamed my mother for him leaving when I was so young. She never would talk to me about him and I blamed her for keeping us apart, when in truth he knew where I was and could have contacted me at any time."

"He was trying to start over. I was only twenty-four when we first met. I'd just started teaching undergrad classes at Temple University and he swept me off my feet," Linda explained.

"Did you know he had a drinking problem?" Holly asked.

Linda nodded. "I did. He was so diligent about attending the AA meetings back then and I admired his determination to beat his addiction. He was so good with Megan when she was a baby, but as time went by I took on more responsibilities at work and he had to pick up the slack at home and with Megan.

"It all became too much, but he never said anything, he just started sneaking a drink here and there. That led him to a complete relapse and he never managed to get completely dry again. He lost his job and I had to work even harder to provide for all three of us. I kept thinking he would get his act together, but it never happened. When Megan was twelve, I decided I owed it to her and myself to live in a household that wasn't controlled by drunken rages and ill-spent money. I kicked him out and filed for divorce. Megan never forgave me for doing that and she never understood that I did it for her as much as for myself. Of course, I also did it for him. I wasn't doing him any favors enabling him the way I was."

"She was a child trying to comprehend a very adult situation. I don't think many kinner can truly understand divorce," Holly recognized.

Linda nodded her head. "I know that, but it doesn't make dealing with it any easier."

Holly gave the woman a smile of sympathy, knowing that in her line of work as a psychologist and professor to young adults, she was fully aware of the impact such things could have on a person.

"I just wish she could understand how much I love her and that I was trying to protect her from him and his lifestyle. I loved her father, but the relationship had grown toxic and my first priority as her mother was to protect her." Linda paused and wiped a tear away. "Why can't she understand that?"

A movement in the bed brought both women's eyes to the injured young woman lying there. Megan's eyes were on her mother and tears leaked from the corners. "I do understand. Mamm. I'm so sorry…"

A Song from the Heart.

Megan looked at her mamm and her schweschder

with tears in her eyes. "What happened?" she asked them both.

Linda held her hand and then looked to Holly for an explanation. Holly met Megan's eyes and told her, "You drove into a tree. Why did you leave in the middle of the night?" she asked, trying to sound more concerned than judgmental.

Megan gingerly shook her head. "I just wanted to get away…"

Linda made a noise and shook her head. "I caused this."

Megan shook her head and looked at her mamm. "No. You didn't cause this. I quit taking my medication when I first came to Holly's…everything was so laid back here that I was hoping I could escape the things that were making me feel sad."

Holly touched her shoulder above the cast. "But you brought them with you."

Megan nodded again. "I guess I was still thinking about things as I did when I was twelve. I blamed you for dad leaving and I shouldn't have. I realize now that you did try to help him, but he didn't want anyone's help. Not even mine."

Linda nodded, tears shining in her eyes. "Your father was a sick man and no matter what kind of help was offered him, he just couldn't resist the pull of the alcohol. I tried for so many years, but after you started noticing things, I couldn't risk you… I had to distance us both from the anger and toxic atmosphere. Can you understand that?"

Megan nodded. "I can, I guess I just wanted what every little girl wants, her daddy."

Holly felt tears sting her eyes, wishing she had just a fraction of the good memories of their daed that Megan had. She felt somewhat cheated, but she also felt very blessed. She watched the two women awkwardly hug and felt tears of happiness sting her eyes. Megan had her relationship with her mamm back. Holly had gained a schweschder, something she'd always secretly longed for. Everything was working out just fine. *Denke, Gott.*

Linda dried her tears and then turned at the sound of a male throat being cleared in the direction of the doorway. She looked at the man and then back to Megan. "Robert..."

Megan extended her good arm towards the doorway. "Please come in."

The tall man entered followed directly by Evan and Becca. The little girl let go of Evan's hand and ran to Holly's side, a bouquet of daisies clutched in her tiny hands. Holly picked her up and Becca eyed Megan's casted arm. "Megan has an owie."

Megan nodded and then grinned at the little girl. "I broke my arm."

Becca was still watching the cast and asked, "Does it hurt?"

Megan shook her head. "Not right now. Are those flowers for me?"

Becca thrust the flowers at her. "They're daisies."

"And beautiful," Megan told her, laying them on the side table.

Linda stepped forward, her hand held by the new man. "Holly, this is Robert. My fiancé."

Holly nodded at the man and then turned to her husband. "This is Evan, my husband, and his niece, Becca."

The two men shook hands and Megan explained quietly that Becca lived with Holly and Evan. Robert walked towards the bed and looked down at Megan with nothing but acceptance and compassion in his eyes. "Megan, your mother and I are getting married in a few weeks."

Megan raised an eyebrow. "I thought the wedding was supposed to be a few weeks ago."

Robert looked at Linda and then back to Megan. "I could see how much your absence was bothering your mother and we decided to wait until you could be there."

Megan started crying. "I'm so sorry. I've been so unfair to you."

"Would you please be part of our wedding?" Robert asked, his arm around her mamm's shoulders. "I don't want to replace the memory of your father, but if you'll let me I'd love to build a relationship with you as your step-father."

Megan nodded her head. "I would love to be there." Robert Cooper was fifty-one years old and a widower. Like Linda, he was a professor at Temple University in their law school, and he had a small law practice just off campus where he helped underprivileged and single parents at a nominal fee. He was a kind and patient man, and Megan couldn't have picked a better husband for her mamm. She'd just been too stubborn to admit that.

Everyone was smiling and crying and, after spending a few more minutes, Evan pulled Becca and Holly from the room with a promise that they would come to Linda's house in a few weeks' time to celebrate their wedding.

On the drive home, Holly couldn't help but see the world as a little brighter place. Love had won out and a familye had been reunited. She smiled down at Becca and then whispered in her ear. When Becca started to sing one of the sacred hymns of their Community, Holly closed her eyes and let herself be swept away by the clear, pure tones. Becca had a lovely voice, and hearing it lifted in praise and thanksgiving to Gott was the most beautiful sound in the world.

When the song was finished, Holly opened her eyes and saw a broad smile on Evan's handsome face. This was her familye and Gott willing, one day they would have another boppli and grow the familye. But until then, she would spend every moment of each day being thankful for Evan and Becca's love and making sure they knew it was returned a thousand-fold.

New Blessings

Three weeks later...

Because Linda lived in Philadelphia, Evan, Becca, and Holly had taken the train into the city. They'd just witnessed Robert and Linda's wedding ceremony and were now headed to Linda's large apartment to celebrate with the happy couple. Megan was almost fully recovered after her car accident. Only the cast still remained set on her arm. Megan had confided in Holly before the ceremony that she was seeing a new doctor who had changed her medication, and she no longer felt as depressed.

Holly was pleased to hear that news and had enjoyed explaining the proceedings of the Christian wedding ceremony to Evan. Becca had been in awe at the many flowers decorating the small church sanctuary, flowers being her favorite thing in the world after Kitty. When Linda had suggested she find some to take home with her, Becca's eyes had lit up and she'd scampered around the small space, picking out the flowers she wanted to keep. Holly knew they would be wilted and pathetic-looking come morning, but Becca wouldn't care.

Evan and she had gotten into a taxi with Becca and, after giving Linda's address to the driver, he'd sat stiffly beside her during the ride. He was unaccustomed to being in an automobile since the Amish rarely used them, only in the case of emergencies. The last time Evan and Holly had been in a moving vehicle had been when she was rushed to hospital on the day she had miscarried their boppli.

Seeing where her thoughts were headed, Holly pushed them aside, choosing to focus on the beautiful couple who were even now welcoming them into their home. "Come in," Linda urged them as they stepped out of the taxi.

Evan paid the fare and then escorted Holly and Becca up the stone steps. They would take the evening train back to Old Repton, but they still had several hours to enjoy the company of Holly's schweschder and celebrate with Linda and Robert.

"You have a lovely home," Holly told them both as they were greeted.

"Thank you. I've asked the caterer to set the table in the dining room and thought we could all eat around the same table, that is, if that is allowed?" Linda asked softly, clearly not wanting to offend Evan or Holly.

Holly smiled at her. "That is fine. It's only during our Sunday church services that we sit apart."

Linda looked relieved. "That's good, I was afraid I

might say or do something wrong that might make you or Evan uncomfortable."

"We're fine and adaptable, you'll see."

"I already can. I'm so glad you were able to come for the wedding. Megan was delighted to see you and has done nothing but talk about coming to visit you during her Fall break."

"We would love to have her come visit then. That is in October?" Holly asked as she followed her hostess into the dining room.

"Yes. She has a four-day weekend and was talking about taking the train up and back."

Holly smiled at Megan who had joined them and appeared to be waiting on an answer. "You are welcome to come visit at any time. I've kind of missed you these last few weeks."

"I've missed you as well," Megan told her, hugging her for a moment. "I wish we could talk on the phone, or..."

"Write. You can write to me and I will write back. It only takes a day for a letter to get from one place to another."

"Really? I don't think I've ever written a letter..." Megan told her, the idea clearly foreign in a world taken up with computers and cell phones.

"I submit all my articles in written format now. You'll find it gets easier with each letter written. I'll be looking forward to receiving your first one in a week or so," Holly told her with a smile.

"I'll do it. It will give me something to do when the professors in my classes become too boring," Megan told her with a giggle, receiving a stern look from her mamm.

"You need to pay attention to your professors…"

"…says the professor," Megan completed the sentence. "I was just kidding. I do pay attention, but I'll find time to write, too."

"Gut! Now, what is that delicious smell coming from the table over there?"

Megan looped her arm through Holly's and pulled her over to sit beside her at the table. "A little bit of everything." Several uniformed servers came into the room and set more dishes on the table and then walked around, filling crystal goblets with water from silver pitchers.

Becca joined them, as did the two men, and soon everyone was eating and enjoying one another's company. It was plain to see that Robert and Linda were deeply in love, and Holly silently rejoiced as she watched them interact with Megan, seeing how much progress the young woman had made since her accident. Megan had decided to give Robert a chance to build a relationship with her and she'd also mended the relationship with her mamm. It was so nice to see, and Holly thanked Gott for healing the familye before her.

Three hours later, Evan, Becca, and Holly boarded the train to head home. Becca had with her a new coloring book and a box of crayons from Linda, and she spent the train trip coloring a picture of two fish-shaped kites.

Evan and Holly sat side-by-side, holding hands and whispering quietly about the day. It had been a blessed day, from the beautiful weather to the words spoken by the pastor as Robert and Linda took their vows.

"Englisch ceremonies are quite different from the Amish way of getting married," Evan remarked.

"Jah. The guests at an Englisch wedding would never sit through a three-hour sermon, let alone more than one of them." Holly tried to imagine any of the co-workers she'd known a year before sitting through one sermon that lasted half an hour, let alone one that lasted all morning long and seemed intent on reminding everyone in attendance how they were supposed to act and be humble. Most of them would get up and walk out of such a service.

"You did," Evan reminded her with a smile.

Holly blushed and nodded her head. "Jah, I did. I used the time to daydream about what our married life was going to be like. Becca kept me from falling asleep."

Evan chuckled, kissed her forehead, and then tucked her close to his side. "We live a gut life."

"We do at that." She settled into his embrace and turned her eyes back to watching Becca color. She did have a wonderful life and had no complaints at the moment. She had wants, but she'd learned to be patient and trust Gott to provide everything that was needed in His perfect timing. Contentment was a key ingredient to being happy, and Holly was pleased at how she'd learned to be content with whatever circumstances she found herself in. Gott had been very gut to her and she made a point each day to remember that.

Evan became absorbed in his own thoughts and

Becca was fully committed to her coloring in. That left Holly free to enjoy people watching. She was fascinated by the people who came and went largely unnoticed during her daily life. Especially in the Englisch world, with its fast pace and seemingly direction-oriented ways. She settled against Evan's shoulder and imagined how the elderly couple sitting further down the carriage had raised their children and sent them off into an uncertain world, content in the knowledge that they had armed them with the morals and education to make the best of the opportunities presented to them as adults. Also in the carriage were a young couple, holding hands and so absorbed in one another that they probably were not even aware of Holly looking at them. They stared into one another's eyes as if all the answers to the world's questions were there for the taking. Caught between the experiences of the two couples, Holly wondered where her life would have taken her had she not followed her mother's origins and taken up the life of an Amish fraa. At the thought she looked across to little Becca and then let her eyes linger up at Evan. She was truly blessed. He smiled down at her and kissed her forehead.

They arrived back at their haus just before 10 o'clock that evening. Evan helped Becca get ready for bed to let Holly retire to bed. Her stomach had begun bothering her an hour earlier and she was not sure if she was getting sick or had just eaten something that didn't agree with her system.

She was lying on their bed when she suddenly bolted upright in the bed. She mentally calculated before getting up and slipping into shoes to head back downstairs to the kitchen. She rummaged in the medical box and then headed outside for a moment. She returned several minutes later with a huge smile on her face.

"I thought you were feeling unwell?" Evan asked her, meeting her in the kitchen as she shut and locked the door behind her.

Holly nodded her head. "I was. Is Becca in bed?"

Evan smiled. "She was asleep the minute her head touched the pillow. It was a long day for a little girl."

Holly nodded and then headed for the stairs, keeping a tight hold on whatever it was that was in her hand. She felt Evan following behind her and it took everything she had to wait until they reached their bedroom and he'd closed the door before she opened her palm and revealed what it was that she held.

Evan looked at the white plastic stick with the two distinct blue lines and then up at her face. He knew without being told what she was trying to tell him, and he swept her up into his arms and turned her around until she squealed and begged him to stop before her sick stomach returned.

"I'm so happy," Holly told him, accepting the kiss he offered her.

"A boppli. Gott has blessed us again today," Evan told her with a huge smile.

Holly nodded and allowed herself to give into the tears of happiness. Evan did his best to calm her down and it was almost an hour before they finally crawled into bed, having spent several long minutes praying to Gott and thanking Him for this new blessing in their lives. They would tell Becca in the morning, and then

Holly would go into town and use the emergency phone to make a doctor's appointment. Evan had been insistent upon it, and Holly knew she would rest much easier if a doctor could assure her there was no danger to the boppli.

She committed to doing everything she could to make sure this pregnancy went to completion, and she dreamed of holding her boppli in her arms, nine months from now.

Seven and a half months later...

Holly was exhausted after twenty-two hours of labor, but as she gazed down at the pink bundle wrapped in her arms, she didn't care. Her little girl had all ten fingers and toes, and a healthy set of lungs. Evan had been a huge source of strength for her, both today and over the months she was plagued daily by morning sickness.

Those days were over now, and she held the beautiful gift of life that Gott had entrusted to her care in her arms. Evan had gone to get Becca from the nurses' station where she'd been patiently waiting during the last few hours of Holly's delivery. The nurses had been very helpful, and Holly hoped Becca and Evan would convey her appreciation.

The door opened, and Evan walked in with Becca holding his hand. The minute she spied Holly holding the boppli, she bolted for the bed, climbed up on the chair nearby, and leaned over to peer at the boppli carefully. The boppli chose to open her blue eyes at that exact moment and the two girls stared at one another, one in wonder at how small her new schweschder was, the other just taking in the new world around her.

"How are you doing?" Evan asked, leaning over the opposite side of the bed for another glimpse of his dochder.

"Tired, but happy," Holly told him.

"She needs a name," he murmured, running a fingertip down a red cheek.

Holly nodded in agreement. "Jah, she does. Did you have something in mind?" For the past several weeks they had been considering all possible names for their new kinner and had finally decided to wait until the boppli was born to choose a name that fit best.

Holly had been convinced she was having a boy, so finding out she'd given birth to a girl had been somewhat of a shock, albeit a gut one.

Evan reached for the boppli and held her close to his chest for a moment before holding her in his large palms and gazing down at her. "I think she should be named after the people who meant so much to us but couldn't be here to see this day."

Holly looked at him and then asked, "What are you thinking?"

Evan looked at her and smiled. "Well, I think she should be called Sarah after your late mamm. But I would also like for her name to reflect her mamm and daed. Can we call her Hope?"

"Hope Sarah," Holly tried out the name, laughing a bit when the boppli gave a cry as if in agreement with the name. "Well, she seems to like that name. What do you think, Becca? Shall we call her Hope Sarah?"

Becca jumped up and down in the chair. "Can I hold Hope Sarah? I'll be very careful."

Holly smiled and nodded, watching as Evan instructed Becca to sit down and then gently placed the newborn in her arms, hovering nearby to rescue them both if need be. She felt tears sting her eyes at the beautiful picture the two girls made together.

Gott had replaced that which had been lost to her and Evan, and all was well. Hope Sarah was perfect, and Holly knew she was only the first of many blessings that would come into their lives as they did their best to live out their faith in Gott and follow His Word. *Denke, Gott.*

Part Three

Finding Faith

Three Years Later

Old Repton, Pennsylvania

Holly Miller peeked into the bedroom where her dochder still lay sleeping. Her baby fine hair was slightly damp where she slept on it and she looked so peaceful and serene. Holly pulled the door partially closed and headed back to the kitchen. She checked on the bread she had left rising on the counter and then poured herself a glass of water. The laundry was already hanging out to dry on the line and she had a few moments in which to relax and just enjoy the day.

She walked out onto the front porch, looking at the sunflowers that she had planted along the border of the flower garden. Where most Amish would have a garden out back of their haus to help provide fresh vegetables for their familye, the Miller farm provided all the fruits and vegetables they needed. Holly liked knowing that Evan was working his land, somewhere fairly close by.

She smiled as a gentle breeze moved the row of sunflowers, showing the colorful bouquet of flowers that rose skyward behind them. The bright yellow flowers with the dark brown centers that were as big as dinner plates were well over six feet tall now. It was mid-August and everything on the farm was maturing and producing well. She loved her life and she never missed an opportunity to tell Gott how blessed she felt. Especially in light of the last two years. They hadn't been easy for her at all. Or for her familye.

Holly had been so excited when she found out she was pregnant again, but the revelation had also brought a healthy dose of internal angst. Having lost her first boppli in the first four months of her pregnancy, she'd been so afraid that history would repeat itself, but Gott had been merciful and three years ago she'd given birth to a healthy baby girl.

Evan and she had named her Hope, her name expressing all of the gratitude and their expectations for the future. And while she'd been the apple of her daed's eye, Holly had struggled with becoming a mamm to a newborn boppli. She'd experienced severe post-partum depression after giving birth, and it had taken several weeks before Evan had even realized things were not as they should be. It had been a slow progression that only seemed to take her further into despair with no light at the end of the tunnel.

Her pregnancy and the changes she'd gone through had been very stressful on her body back then and she'd struggled to find a way to be happy. The hormones rushing through her body, combined with a lack of sleep and the overwhelming fear that had plagued her pregnancy had taken their toll. Depression had sucked the very life energy from her and she'd felt almost no connection to her infant dochder in those first few months.

Oh, she'd tried. She'd gone through the motions that she thought were expected of her, being a new mamm and all, but as days rolled into one another, she seemed to slow down. She found herself crying uncontrollably at times, and at other times too tired to even crawl from her bed. She hid what was happening from her husband for a few weeks, but then her illness became too severe to keep hidden. Once Evan had figured out what was happening, he and Becca, the niece he'd taken in after her parents had been killed in a haus fire, had done their best to help Holly.

They'd shouldered more of the farm work, a necessity since there were many days ahead when getting out of bed had been very hard for Holly. Evan had been very understanding and supportive, and his love for her had never faltered. He'd prayed with her, and when he'd had to tend the farm fields, Becca was there lending her moral and physical support. Other women from their Community helped by preparing food, taking over some household chores, and just sitting with Holly and reading to her from the Bible. As the weeks passed by, with everyone's loving support, she gradually got better.

Symptoms of postpartum depression are similar to what happens normally following childbirth. While it is not uncommon for any mom to experience baby blues, Holly was of the few whose depression escalated. The baby blues include difficulty sleeping, change in appetite, sublime levels of fatigue, and frequent mood changes. Holly went through all that but as time went on, instead of unwrapping herself from these symptom as they eased off in the natural course of events, hers were accompanied by other symptoms of major depression. These are not normal after childbirth, and included loss of pleasure, depressed moods, thoughts harmful to herself and others and unnatural feelings of worthlessness, hopelessness, and helplessness. The doctors were surprised that she had fallen prey to this disabling disease since she was not considered to fall within the categories at risk.

Factors than can increase the risk of postpartum depression include ambivalence during the pregnancy, a past history of depression, lack of support, isolation, and marital conflict. Younger moms are also at higher risk as are moms who already have children. Holly had to agree that she was one of the few who had slipped through the cracks to suffer this onslaught of sadness which brought out elements not associated with the wunderbaar mamm she hoped to be.

Evan was overwhelmed by the change in his beloved Holly during this time. He had seen her struggle with the loss of their unborn boppli, only to come out even stronger. After anticipating the joy of finally holding the life they had created together through their love and the blessings of a Fatherly Gott, he often could not stand to see Holly show no affection for little Hope. He knew that the depression had robbed him of the true and living Holly and he recognized that this parallel being would let go of the hold she had on his wife and the mamm to his dochder in Gott's good time. When that happened he would be there to welcome her back. Until then Evan planned to be the supportive husband Holly needed to see her through this dark time. He would be both Mamm and Daed to Hope until Holly made it out of the black tunnel of hopelessness that had swallowed her so entirely.

Holly's column in the paper should have suffered during this time, but just the opposite proved to be true. Her editor made a trip to Old Repton to visit her, and he was very understanding, making sure her readers knew she would be back. Holly had gained so much popularity with her readers, they'd been more than willing to wait for her to start writing again. Holly again surprised her doctor who had made it very clear that she would have to enter into therapy as a means to treat the postpartum depression, when she proved that writing about the affliction in her column was all the therapy she needed. By being candid about her experience, she not only helped other women suffering similarly but also the faceless others who might be helped in the future through reading about her struggles.

Now that she was over that part of her life, she felt very grateful for having experienced all those feelings and emotions. It gave her another avenue to connect with her readers. Holly's column, when she resumed writing, became even more popular and soon several newspapers were printing her experiences.

In addition to writing about her life as a wife in the Amish community, she was able to write about life as a mamm and the struggles she faced. This new perspec-

tive on motherhood was not at all as she had ever expected, and she enjoyed reliving moments in her stories.
Holly never withheld talking about Gott and her devo-
tion to His ways when writing her column. She prayed
that through her words, other women might get the help
they needed to persevere in times of great struggle. She
believed that Englisch women could benefit from the
same lessons she was learning as an Amish one.

The newspapers insisted on running her photo alongside her column, and Holly had become accustomed to
having strangers come up to her, mostly Englischers,
telling her how much they loved reading her column.
Holly liked that people felt a connection to her, but it
was the mamms who praised her for her bravery in
speaking about her depression and writing openly about
how she'd relied on Gott to help her, that made all the
obstacles she'd encountered worthwhile.

Holly's relationship with Gott had grown so much
through that time, and she loved how close she felt to
Him now. He'd also allowed her relationship with Evan
and with Becca to grow and most days Holly never even
thought about the fact that Becca wasn't her biological
dochder. She'd been Becca's mamm for all intents and
purposes since the little girl was five years old and she
could no longer imagine not having her in her life.

Now that she'd overcome her depression, she found
it very new and refreshing to be a mamm and to learn
about her dochder day by day. She hadn't fully understood all the sacrifices and hard work her own mamm
had gone through to provide for her, but now she did.
Her mother was no longer alive, but Holly constantly

gave a silent prayer of thanks for her sacrifices. Sacrifices that had been made out of love and that she now was making for her own kinners. But with those sacrifices came great blessings and joy.

Evan's farm had also developed over the years and he'd been blessed to be able to purchase adjacent land and expand the enterprise. So much so that he had hired five more men to help him with the farming. He had also expanded the types of produce he grew. They now had several orchards of trees bearing a variety of fruit, and extensive fields of vegetables. The expansion had been very successful.

In addition to providing produce for the local farmer's market, he now supplied several grocery stores in surrounding towns with all manner of fresh produce. He'd even hired several young men from the Community to be delivery drivers. Instead of their small buggies, he'd purchase several large wagons, some covered and some not, and twice a week they were loaded up and driven to the stores they supplied. His fruits and vegetables were always fresh and picked before they were too ripe, and he credited Gott with blessing his endeavors. The Englischers outside Old Repton praised him for his quality products, but Evan was always careful to give all the praise and glory to Gott. That was the Amish way.

Returning Nightmare

The sound of Hope waking from her nap brought Holly back into the haus. Her little dochder was growing up so quickly and it seemed Holly was able to identify changes in her almost daily. Her hair had finally come in, and the baby fine blonde locks now curled around her angelic face, damp with sweat from where she'd laid upon them during her nap. She was adorable, and Holly kissed her on the forehead as she picked her up. She quickly changed her wet diaper. They were working on becoming diaper free, but so far, remaining dry while asleep, whether in the form of a nap or at night, was proving beyond her dochder's control.

"How's my darling?" Holly kept up a soft one-sided dialogue with Hope. Once she was dry again, she cuddled her against her shoulder and headed for the kitchen. She set her on the counter and poured her a glass of the day's fresh milk, grabbing one of the oatmeal cookies she'd made the day before as well and handing it to Hope. "Shall we go see what Becca is up to?" she asked, smiling when Hope nodded and reached for her once more.

Hope was growing up quickly, but there were times when she still wanted to be held and cuddled like the little girl she was. Holly complied, grateful for these moments to savor her dochder's affection. The same could be said for Becca. She was also growing up so quickly, and as Holly settled into the wooden rocking chair, she observed her from the porch. Becca was growing up and there were very few reminders of the little girl Holly had first come to know. Everything and everyone around her was maturing, which was neither gut nor bad—it simply was life.

She heard the sound of Becca's voice coming from the yard and she turned her head and watched while Becca played with the barnyard kittens. A new litter had been born several weeks earlier, and they were just beginning to explore their surroundings. At the age of nine, Becca was finally coming into her own. The kittens had become her new charges and she talked to them as they followed her around the yard, their mamm watching carefully from her perch on a nearby fence post.

When Holly first met Becca she had been a mute for some time, refusing to speak to anyone since the death of her parents months earlier. Holly still didn't understand why, but Becca had seen something in her that she trusted, and she'd started speaking once more. Now, almost four years later, Becca was no longer shy and quiet, but quite gregarious and always open to meeting new friends.

She had a lovely singing voice and had joined the

youth choir. Holly and Evan never failed to enjoy listening to her sing at their Sunday services. She was such an angel and had been tremendously helpful when Hope was first born. She did well in her school studies and Holly thanked Gott that the young girl seemed to have overcome her past trauma.

Holly watched her for a few moments, noticing that something about Becca seemed off. She seemed overly tired, almost lethargic as she played with the kittens, and Holly worried that she might be coming down with an illness. She carried Hope down the porch steps and called to Becca, "Dochder, come here."

"Mamm?" Becca asked moments later, presenting herself with two kittens, one held in each hand.

Holly smiled at her. "Is everything alright?"

Becca hesitated only a moment before nodding. "Jah."

Holly cocked her head to the side and shook her head. "You look tired. Are you feeling ill?"

Becca set the kittens down and shook her head. "Nee. I'm not sick."

Holly sat down on the porch steps and gestured for Becca to join her. "Something is bothering you?"

Becca waited for a long moment and then she slowly nodded. "Jah."

Holly laid a hand on her shoulder. "Tell me what it is."

Becca looked up at her with a worried look on her face. "I didn't want to worry you and Daed." Holly was not yet over being surprised whenever little Becca referred to her and Evan as Mamm and Daed. It had been a blessing and indicated the little orphaned girl's full acceptance of them as her parents.

Holly was becoming worried. She let Hope down on the grass and then turned to look at Becca. "Please talk to me."

Becca nodded. "The dreams…they're back."

Holly's eyes widened. "You are having nightmares again?"

"Jah."

"For how long?" Holly wanted to know. She made an effort to keep her voice perfectly calm, but inside her heart was breaking for Becca.

"A few weeks," she looked up, worry evident on her face.

"Oh, sweetie. Why didn't you say something to us?" Becca had suffered nightmares after her parents' deaths, but she'd been very young and unable to articulate what was in them. She'd stopped having them after a while and both Evan and Holly had been much relieved. They'd been praying along with other members of their Community that Gott would deliver Becca from the nightmares, and they'd given Gott all of the thanks when she'd finally started sleeping through the night without waking up in tears and terrified. *But now they're back? Why? Gott, please help me.*

"I thought maybe they would go away." Becca was looking at the ground and Holly's heart went out to the little girl.

She softened her voice even more. "Becca, can you tell me about the dream?"

Becca nodded her head. "They're always the same.

The house is on fire… I can feel the heat from the flames. My bedroom is filling with smoke and it's hard to breathe."

Holly nodded her head, these images and feelings were to be expected, given the fact that Becca had woken up in her haus when it was engulfed in flames. "Anything else?"

Becca nodded her head. "There's a woman."

"A woman?" This is new. Her mamm? But her parents hadn't made it out of their bedroom that night.

"At the door to my bedroom. I can see her face, but when I wake up it's hard to remember it exactly."

"Do you recognize her?" Holly asked.

Becca shook her head. "Nee. It wasn't my mamm."

Holly nodded and then asked the next obvious question. "What is the woman doing?"

"Watching me. She has a horrible look on her face and I can tell she doesn't like me."

Holly wasn't quite sure what to make of Becca's dream. "Well, I'm not sure what it means, but I want you to come wake us up the next time you have it. Okay?"

Becca nodded and then stood up to play with Hope. She brought one of the kittens over and let Hope pet the soft fur. Holly watched her dochders playing for a few minutes and then asked Becca to watch Hope while she went in search of Evan. She needed to tell him what Becca had just shared with her and check whether her dream might make more sense to him.

Why is Becca dreaming of another woman being in the haus on the night of the fire? Evan had never mentioned anything about that before. What could it mean?

First Concern

Several weeks later...

Becca left the small schulhaus in the center of town, waving to her friends as she headed for the farmer's market at the top end of Main street. The market was open today and she knew that Holly and Hope would be helping Evan with their produce tables. She looked up when she came to the corner, looking both ways before crossing, and then paused when she spied the strange woman lurking behind a flower cart several shops up the street.

Becca watched her for a moment, wondering why she kept seeing this woman. For the last few days, this woman seemed to be wherever Becca was, and she almost always seemed to be staring at her. Her presence and staring gave Becca a weird feeling that was more bad that gut. *Who is she? Is she watching me or am I just imagining that she is? Am I being paranoid?* This was a new word she'd recently learned to spell, and she smiled to herself that she'd found a way to use it appropriately, even if it was only inside her head.

Becca crossed the street and was not even shocked to see the woman doing the same only moments later. Deciding to confront the woman, she turned and waited for the woman to look at her, locking her gaze with her own. Becca could not help but take a step backwards in response to the blank look in the strange woman's eyes. Becca was very mature for her age, having experienced more tragedy in her young life than many adults ever would.

Becca finally broke her gaze and headed for the open-air market at the end of the street. She gave a thought to mentioning the woman to Evan and Holly but saw how busy they both were once she arrived at the market. How busy they always were. Holly and Evan worked so hard. She didn't want to worry them, especially given the fact that the nightmares had already served to do just that.

A few weeks earlier, when Becca had finally come clean and told Holly that the nightmares were back, Holly had immediately gone out to the barn to find Evan. He'd been worried and had abandoned the day's chores to spend the day with her, trying to help her deal with what was happening. The unidentified woman was very concerning to everyone, and Becca could almost describe her, but some of her features always remained a little hazy when Becca woke up.

She paused at the edge of the market and glanced over her shoulder, seeing the woman peeking out from around the corner of a store front, looking right at her. Becca felt shivers run down her back, but after considering burdening Evan and Holly with more concerns, she decided to just keep things to herself for now. The woman hadn't really done anything wrong. She was obviously an Englischer…*maybe she just thinks I look like someone else?*

Becca turned back and put a smile on her face. Holly needed help and she wanted to see Hope. She forced thoughts of the strange woman aside and quickly made her way over to the familye's tables. "Can I help?"

Holly turned with a warm smile. "Jah. Can you get me a ten-pound bag of potatoes for this lady?"

Becca nodded, thankful for something to do. "Jah. I can do that."

"Denke, Becca. How was school?"

"Gut. The choir practiced again."

Holly touched her shoulder. "I cannot wait to hear you."

Becca nodded and then grabbed the bag of potatoes, pulling it over to the table and smiling when Holly reached down to help lift it up for their customer. While Holly finished helping the Englischer, Becca looked around for something else to do. Her eyes fell on Hope playing in a small enclosure which Evan had built for her in between the market tables. Becca walked over and climbed inside with her. She loved her schweschder and given how much of a burden she'd been over the past few years, she welcomed any opportunity to help take care of her for Holly. She was helping, and it felt very gut to know that she was doing something for Holly instead of the other way around.

Holly placed her hands on her lower back and then arched, stretching her muscles after a long day of being on her feet. Once again, the farmer's market had been very successful, and she smiled at the man who helped with their farm work as they began to pack away the produce and fruit that hadn't sold yet. Tomorrow they would do the same thing all over again, but Evan would be there to help. Today, he'd accompanied the delivery carts to the grocery stores in a nearby town and would meet her back at their haus by the time everything was packed away for the night.

She glanced over and saw that Becca had finally put Hope to sleep. Becca was sitting on a padded pillow, leaning back against several crates, with Hope draped across her lap. She started to turn away, but the pensive look on Becca's face stopped her. Something was still bothering her.

She put down the list in her hands and walked over, snagging a crate on which to sit on her way over. She sat down and spoke quietly to Becca. "Are you still having the nightmares?"

Becca glanced up and shrugged her shoulders. "Not so much. I mostly wake up before they go too far."

"That is gut."

Becca nodded, but the pensive look was still there. Holly watched her for a moment and then asked, "Is something else bothering you?"

Becca shook her head. "Nee. I'm just tired today."

Holly wanted to believe her, but her maternal intuition told her that something else was causing the little girl some concern. Even though Becca had said she was fine, Holly suspected otherwise.

As soon as she had a moment alone with Evan, she told him about her suppositions. "I can't put my finger on it, but something else is bothering her. She said she wasn't being bothered by the nightmares as much, but the look on her face this afternoon was… I don't know…confused and worried."

Evan's face fell. "I'm sorry. I've been so busy with the farm, I've been neglecting the familye."

Holly shook her head. "Nee. You mustn't feel that way."

"But I do," he told her, reaching for her hand. They were sitting together on the front porch, on the double rocker. He had an arm around her shoulders. Hope had been bathed, fed, and was asleep for the night, and Becca was also tucked up in bed for the night. This was normally their quiet time together during which they would discuss what they had accomplished during the day, pray together about whatever was concerning them, and make plans for the next day.

Holly squeezed his hand. "Everything you've done has been for our future and that of our kinners. You cannot do more than you have been doing."

"Nevertheless, I will pay closer attention to you, Becca, and Hope. My first priority is to my familye and then to the farm."

Holly nodded and then snuggled into his embrace. Whatever was going on with Becca, Evan would investigate. Holly was confident that he would do what he could to set Becca's mind at ease. He was a gut daed and husband. It was at times like these that she gave extra thanks to Gott for bringing him into her life.

Devastation

One week later...

Even though Evan was spending more time around the haus, he hadn't yet been able to pinpoint what was bothering Becca. She insisted that everything was fine, and he and Holly had decided to give her some space in the hope that she would come to them with whatever was giving her cause for concern. It was all they could do at the time, especially given the disasters that kept befalling the farm.

It all began two days earlier. The tomatoes and peppers were scheduled to be harvested at the end of the week. When Evan went out to conduct a final inspection on the plants, however, he was dismayed to see that the fields had been good and properly trampled, the fruit ruined, and the plants broken off at the ground. The entire crop of tomatoes and peppers were a total loss!

Evan had returned to the haus, fighting back tears of frustration and anger as he tried to understand what could have happened. Visible footprints had been left behind by the perpetrators of this cruel crime, but he had a hard time imagining anyone carrying out such a vile deed.

The next day at the Sunday meeting, he raised the problem before the entire Community, asking whoever was responsible to please come forward so that forgiveness could be given after an apology was offered. No one came forward. Evan had returned from that Sunday meeting depressed and finding it hard to stay in the right frame of mind.

Holly did her best to help him, but nothing like this had ever happened before in their small town. The manner in which every single plant had been destroyed was evidence of a deep rage and anger against Evan's familye by whoever had carried out the deed. It was very concerning for everyone.

On Monday matters got much worse. Evan was finishing the breakfast Holly had prepared for him when two of his workers arrived at the kitchen door, their hats in their hands, tears on their faces, and looks of complete horror in their eyes.

"What is wrong?" he demanded, his heart beating quickly.

"The horses…"

"What about the horses?" Evan asked, dreading the answer just by the looks on their faces.

"They're all dead. Someone poisoned them. They have blood coming out of their noses and mouths… Who would do such a thing?"

Evan staggered backwards through the doorway, his face draining of all color. "Someone killed the horses?"

"Jah."

Holly gasped, shocked at such violence amongst the Amish. Evan took great care of his horses and for someone to have killed them all was beyond reprehensible! Evan stepped back inside the haus, made his way over to a chair, and sat for a minute. He looked up at Holly with tears running down his face. "Why is this happening? First the crops. Now, the horses. My horses. Why am I being sabotaged so cruelly?"

"Sabotage?" Holly repeated, coming to sit down beside him.

Evan nodded. "What else could it be?"

Holly shook her head. "I don't know, but this is frightening, Evan."

Evan pulled her up as he stood and hugged her tightly. "With Gott's help, we will get through this. I will start locking the barn, and the men and I will keep watch for intruders."

Holly nodded, wishing there was something more she could do, but she had two little girls to take care of. The best she could do for the immediate time being was to take care of the haus and the kinners.

"Should we call the authorities?" she asked as Evan prepared to inspect the horses for himself.

Evan turned on her, angry at the situation. "And tell them what? We don't have any idea who did this."

Holly knew he wasn't mad at her, but he'd never spoken to her in that tone of voice before. "It was just a suggestion…"

Evan sighed and gave her an apologetic look. "I'm sorry I barked at you. This situation is untenable."

Holly went to him and hugged him. "I'm sorry about the horses."

Evan held her for a moment and then set her back. "I'll go see if I can figure out what kind of poison was used. I'll put the word out and ask everyone in the Community to keep their eyes open for any other mischief."

Evan and his men buried the horses, and the effect of the loss on the farm was devastating. Luckily theirs was a community that helped one another, and several neighbors brought horses over for them to use. Evan was grateful but refused to keep the horses at his farm overnight, afraid more tragedy might befall them.

But it wasn't to be the horses that his attacker went after two days later. Even though he now locked the barn and other outbuildings, and his men were taking turns keeping guard over the farm at night, the attacker still managed a successful nefarious act.

He woke up on Wednesday morning to the sounds of Holly screaming for him from the yard. He rushed from their bedroom, still buttoning up his shirt and with only his socks on his feet. Holly stood in front of the chicken coops, surrounded by the dead bodies of more than a dozen chickens. The remaining chickens, still in their cages, were squawking loudly, distressed by whatever had happened to their fellow feathered friends.

"Holly, come here," Evan called to her, wanting to get her back into the haus and away from the sight of the carnage in the yard. She came to him, walking into his arms and sobbing against his chest. He did his best to calm her down and was grateful when a worker arrived and offered to take care of cleaning up the yard.

"Denke. I'm going to take care of Holly…"

"You do what you need to do," the mann told him and Evan nodded, anger and disbelief stealing his voice for the moment.

He was glad that Becca and Hope were still asleep inside the haus. Becca had such a tender heart, she didn't need to see this latest disaster. She'd already been asking questions about the horses, and Evan had chosen to ignore her questions rather than explain how someone had purposely killed them. How did one explain such a vile act to someone so young? As an adult, he didn't even understand.

Holly busied herself in the haus by making a fresh pot of kaffe, drying her tears and trying to still her shaking hands. Evan was pacing back and forth, his anger palpable. He was talking to himself, or maybe to Gott… she was having a hard time figuring out which. He was angry and making no secret of that fact.

She pulled herself together, drawing upon a well of patience she normally reserved for the girls. Now it was her turn to be there for Evan. She'd been praying daily for Evan since the destruction of the crops, and now she looked out the kitchen window and uttered a whispered plea.

"Gott, You know how hard Evan works. I don't understand why this is happening or what part these disasters could have in Your plan for our lives… Things have been going so well, and now it seems there is a new disaster almost every day.

"Please help Evan and me to see what Your plan is and guide Evan as he tries to make decisions in regard to the farm.

"Gott, please help me be patient with his anger and be a source of comfort for him. Whatever is going on here, please help us. Please put a stop to these needless and senscless attacks."

Mystery Woman

Becca stood in the doorway to the kitchen, her eyes looking back and forth between Evan and Holly. Holly was standing at the kitchen window praying quietly beneath her breath. Evan was pacing angrily and talking to Gott and he sounded like he was very angry. Angry with Gott? Why?

She walked towards Holly and waited until Holly had spotted her before asking, "Why is Evan mad at Gott?"

Holly looked at her husband and then shook her head. "He's not mad at Gott, but with the situation."

"What situation?" Becca asked.

Evan stopped pacing and faced her. "You asked me what happened to the horses?" When Becca nodded, he explained, "Someone poisoned them."

"What?!" Becca asked, shocked at what she was hearing.

"They also destroyed the tomato and pepper crops, and last night…" he paused, trying to gain control of his emotions. Once he accomplished that, to the best of his ability given the circumstances, he addressed the latest attack. "Last night they killed half of our chickens."

Becca shook her head, fearful and saddened by what she was hearing. "Why? Who did these things?"

Holly came to her, shaking her head. "We don't know."

Becca had a bad feeling that the strange woman who kept following her might have something to do with all these tragedies. The woman had followed her home from school last week, making sure she kept just far enough away that Becca couldn't really see her. She battled with herself, knowing she probably needed to say something, but not wanting to add to either of their burdens.

She grew quiet for so long, she didn't realize that Evan and Holly were both watching her carefully.

"What's going on, Becca?" Evan asked, holding her gaze and demanding with his eyes that she come clean.

Becca looked at Holly, but there was no help coming from that quarter either. Her time for keeping silent was over. "There's this woman…"

"What woman?" Evan demanded.

"The woman who's been following me."

Evan shook his head and grabbed her hand, pulling her over to sit at the table. "Someone has been following you?" When Becca nodded, he asked. "For how long?"

"Several weeks." She could see that this information was upsetting to both her parents and she hurried to explain, "I didn't want to worry you. You've both been so busy… I kept thinking she would go away. But she didn't…and now… I think maybe she had something to do with everything bad that's been happening at the farm and to our livestock."

"Why do you think that?" Holly asked.

"She followed me here last week."

Holly and Evan shared a look and then Evan nodded. "We're going to the police. Becca, go find your shoes. Holly, I wish you would come with us."

Holly nodded. "I'll go get Hope up and be ready to go shortly."

"Becca, bring your shoes in here and put them on while you finish telling me about this woman."

Becca hurried to find her shoes and then put them on while Evan watched. "So firstly I want you to understand that no matter how busy Holly and I may seem, we will always have time for you. I'm saddened that you didn't feel like you could come to us with something that was obviously bothering you. I would like you to promise me that it will not happen again."

Becca nodded and then threw herself into his arms. "I'm sorry."

"Shush." Evan hugged her close, and she wrapped her arms around him, holding on tightly and realizing that she'd made a mistake in not telling the two people she considered to be her parents about the woman. There was something very familiar about the woman, but Becca was sure she didn't know the woman's name. Why did she then feel as if she had seen her before? Before she showed up in Old Repton?

Evan patted her back and then set her away from him. "When we get to the police station I want you to answer all their questions. They will want you to describe this woman and tell them where you've seen her. Don't hide anything from them."

"Nee, I wouldn't do that. I promise."

"Gut." Evan looked up as Holly returned to the

kitchen with Hope in her arms. His dochder was still sleepy as was evident by the way she cuddled against her mamm's shoulder. "Gutentag, Hope."

"She's not quite ready to wake up. Why don't you and Becca go into town and I will wait here with Hope?"

Evan ran a hand down Hope's baby fine hair and nodded. "We will do that. Let the menner take care of the chickens…"

Holly nodded. "I will have them see if any of the meat can be salvaged…"

Evan shook his head. "Nee! I don't want to be wasteful, but I couldn't eat anything this person touched. If this woman is responsible for all this… I'm worried what she might do next. I'm going to speak to Thomas and see if he can stay around the haus until I return."

Holly didn't argue the matter, knowing she would feel better knowing that she was not alone and that someone was outside the haus and looking out for her and Hope while Evan was in town. "Jah. Denke."

Evan kissed her on the head and then turned and reached for Becca's hand. "Come. We will go to town and come back as soon as possible." He escorted her from the haus, with Holly watching him from the kitchen door.

He called Thomas over and spoke with him briefly, thanking him when the mann offered the use of his buggy and horse for their trip into town. The five men he'd hired had been very helpful in clearing up after the devastation that had been heaved upon the farm, and today was no different. All the beheaded chickens had been gathered together and placed in a pile. They would be taken out to a safe area and their bodies burned. Thomas agreed to stick close to the haus and Evan shook hands with him before lifting Becca up into the borrowed buggy and heading for town.

The drive was made in silence, Evan's anger rising as he thought about the damage this woman might have done to his farm and his familye. Becca sat by his side, her hands in her lap, and a very worried look upon her normally smiling face. He reached over and squeezed her hands briefly. "Do not worry, Dochder. Gott is still in control."

Becca nodded. "Jah, this I know. What I don't understand is why a stranger would want to hurt the farm?"

"That is what we are going to ask the police to find out."

The local authorities were very concerned when they heard Evan and Becca's story. Especially the fact that this woman had been following Becca around town and had even followed her back to the farm.

"Mr. Miller, I can assure you that we will do everything we can to find this woman. Your daughter was able to give the sketch artist a pretty good idea of what the suspect looks like, although she seemed confused about the woman's facial features."

Evan and the officer looked over to where Becca sat in the big leather chair, her face pale and scared. "She couldn't remember what her face looked like?" Evan questioned.

"No. In fact, the artist said that she became very agitated after thinking about it for a minute. Is there something else she left out?"

Evan pursed his lips and then called Becca over to him. "Dochder, come here." When she was standing in front of him, he softened his voice and asked,

"Becca, have you remembered something else about this woman? Something you are afraid to share?"

Becca looked up at him and shook her head. "Nee, but…"

"Jah? Continue."

"I feel like I should remember her, but I'm sure I don't know her."

"Could you have seen her at the market?" Evan asked, that being one of the few places Becca had plenty of interaction with the Englisch.

"I don't think so," she murmured quietly. "I just don't know."

The officer waved his hand. "Calm yourself, child. We'll find her if she's still in Old Repton or in any of the surrounding towns. I'll see that everyone has a copy of the artist's sketch. I'm also going to make sure we have an officer placed in the vicinity of your farm until things are settled."

Evan tightened his lips and nodded his head. Normally, he wouldn't welcome the local authorities and their motorized vehicles spending time around his farm, but events were escalating quickly and his familye's safety had to come first. He would speak to his neighbors, too, and he knew that they would also help keep a look out for the mystery woman and whoever it was who was creating such havoc on his farm. One way or another, this woman would be found and, if she had anything to do with these crimes, Evan hoped he would find answers to the questions he and the others had.

What the Woman Wants

Maxine Simpson was the type of school girl no one paid much attention to. She was always just there but never quite seen to the extent that she was noticed. She just did not seem at all noteworthy or memorable to her peers or the members of her community. She was never asked out by boys and while she did have girl friends at school, her friendships never lasted very long. She would attach herself very firmly to the friends she did manage to make to the exclusion of everyone else. The problems would arise when Maxine became jealous of whatever other friendships her one and only friend at any given time would have. She would demand exclusivity and pressurize her friends into not mixing with anyone but her. It was not difficult to see why her friendships were always short lived. Her teenage years were therefore defined by loneliness punctuated by periods of isolation. Her parents were both career oriented and fulfilled the expectations of society by producing the one child. Love was never an integral part of her existence. Although her parents most certainly did love Maxine, they overpowered loving and acceptance with high expectations. Maxine was expected to outperform on whatever level possible. When she showed no aptitude for athletics or sport, she was pushed wholeheartedly into academics. Her mother once joked at a family gathering in the presence of Maxine that she might have made an exceptional cheerleader, given her long legs and slim torso, had she only had the slightest inclination towards physical dexterity. Also she added that cheerleaders were expected to have pretty hair and the looks to match. Maxine hunched her shoulders and verily slinked her sixteen-year-old self from the crowded room to the mirth of virtually her entire extended family. She never was cognizant of her dress before, and that one comment from her mother in front of all those people who were meant to love and accept her for who she was caused her from that day on to dress to draw attention away from her long legs and slim torso. She wore nondescript dresses designed to make her appear as frumpish as possible. With dresses worn to below her knees with dropped waistlines in browns and beige, Maxine began to walk with a hunched back, her chin tucked into her chest and her shoulders drooped to appear shorter and attract less attention.

All that she achieved though with her new look was to invite the scorn and ridicule of her peers. She went from unnoticed to condescended very swiftly indeed. All she had left in the final years of her high school career was her intelligence. She swore that no one would ever take that away from her and put all her efforts into achieving top marks in all her subjects at school. She entered academic competitions and eisteddfods, and by the time she graduated she had the recognition of many top tertiary education establishments across the country. She soon had offers of scholarships from all the colleges and universities she admired and had her pick of degrees. Maxine sifted through all the scholarship acceptances she had received before deciding on the one farthest from her home town. So it was that she spent the next chapter of her young life at the University of North Carolina, Chapel Hill, which so happened to be the top-rated school of Pharmacy in the country. At the UNC Eshelman School of Pharmacy on Chapel Hill campus she applied herself one hundred percent to the clinical Doctor of Pharmacy practice degree (Pharm.D.). The degree allowed her entry into the profession and practice of pharmacy. This professional degree curriculum required her to undergo the minimum of two years of study to satisfy prerequisite requirements, which she completed in just one semester at the General College. It was unprecedented, and at just seventeen Maxine was permitted to proceed with what should have been four years of professional coursework. As a graduate of the Pharm.D. program less than three years later, Maxine sat for the state licensure examination for pharmacists. She graduated cum laude and top of her class before she turned twenty, without being able to tell you the name of just one of the students she had spent the better part of her adult life living and studying alongside. She had closed her mind to people and their judgments and had come out on top. That was what she took from Chapel Hill besides her qualification. That and a honed understanding of the social element of the human species of which she had no interest at all in being a part. Along with her qualification came a string of job offers from all across the country. It was inexplicable therefore that the young Maxine landed up in Mercer County, Pennsylvania working as the underling of a soon to be retired pharmacist who had spent his entire working life in this one pharmacy which catered largely to the local Amish contingent. Old Mr. Spiers, the pharmacist, had no family, having never married. What he did have was a business that did very well thank you, a fully paid for luxuriously furnished house and a superb understanding of the Amish people and their ways. The Amish community had a great respect for the old pharmacist which was wholly reciprocated.

Maxine took the position having been lured by the prospect of being trained by an old-school professional with high morals and intact ethics. Mr. Spiers greatest attraction though was his acceptance of a people largely misunderstood by everyone. She figured that if he could live alongside the Amish, he could accept her as she was. She had no intention of changing who she was for anyone and if she could be assured acceptance without condition, she would be more than happy living and working in the far-flung regions out of the way of the lofty and fashionable masses. It was during her time working under the old man that she first met Jacob Yoder.

* * *

Jacob was born and raised on his familye's farm very near to the village of Volant in Pennsylvania. The village itself was originally a small gristmill town that was incorporated in 1893 and is situated adjacent to Old Repton. The Yoder familye, along with the full contingent of Amish residents and farmers in the surrounding area watched as Volant almost became a ghost town in the late 1970s when the mill was shut down. Fortunately during the next decade Volant was revived and restored by interested businessmen. It went on to become the contemporary Volant where Amish buggies co-mingle with modern motor cars in the village's main street. The old gristmill became an attraction as it now stands as a country, antique, and specialty shop. It shared its place on Main Street with shops selling homemade arts and crafts, Victorian collectibles, pottery, Christmas specialties, music-related items, and modern fashion wear. What Volant did not have was a pharmacy, and so the residents of the general area were more than happy to travel the short distance to have Mr. Spiers supply them with all they needed on the medicinal front that could not be made in their homes and passed down through generations.

Jacob Yoder suffered with asthma. He required his monthly supply of a fresh cartridge for his asthma pump and for this he visited Mr. Spiers almost religiously. He had to admit to being surprised to see the young lady in the white coat behind the prescription counter when he popped into the pharmacy that Fall day to collect his usual. No one had ever known anyone but Mr. Spiers to be there.

* * *

Maxine heard the bell chime over the entrance door to the pharmacy and she straightened herself into standing position from her position kneeling down behind the dispensing counter where she was unpacking a delivery of pharmaceuticals. A young man stood in the pharmacy, looking over the new display of men's razors. Maxine caught herself thinking. "He doesn't need razors, just look at that thick growth of beard on his chin."

Jacob looked up at that moment and Maxine imagined that he was drawn by her inner thoughts of him.

"Hello," Jacob said unassumingly. "I'm sorry but I was hoping to see Mr. Spiers for my asthma inhaler refill."

No sooner had Jacob said hello to the young lady than Mr. Spiers appeared from the consulting room at the back. He introduced the two.

"Maxine, Jacob Yoder is a regular monthly visitor to our establishment. Once a month he comes in to collect the asthma pump refill he has on a repeat prescription. Jacob, this is Maxine Simpson. She is to help me in the store from now on and one day when I am no longer here, she will be running the pharmacy just as well if not better than I ever did."

Jacob asked the young Maxine many questions about her origin and where she had been schooled.

"So, you are not from these parts then," Jacob commented when she told him where she had grown up and been schooled before going onto university in North Carolina.

Maxine knew that she was blushing when she answered Jacob. "No. I am new to these parts. Had I known that such beauty and serenity existed within America, perhaps I might have landed up here much sooner than I did."

"Be that as it may, I am quite sure that Mr. Spiers is very fortunate to have you working for him. It was very gut to make your acquaintance, Miss Simpson, and I have no doubt I will be seeing you again in a month's time, if not sooner. Gutentag, Mr. Spiers, Miss Simpson."

She was bowled over by his attentiveness and that was where the trouble began.

It was many months before Maxine found out that Ruth Yoder even existed. By the time she did though, she was well and truly obsessed with Jacob. She had asked him so many questions that she imagined that she had been a part of his life for years. In her mind, she and Jacob started courting very soon after they met that first day in the pharmacy. She believed fully that Jacob had every intention of asking her to marry him just as soon as he plucked up the courage to do so.

When Maxine took a stroll through the green areas of the town and saw Jacob driving his buggy down the Main Street that blustery Fall day, she was visibly aghast that he shared the seat with a young lady who was clearly in the family way. When she returned to the pharmacy, she tried as nonchalantly as possible to find out from Spiers who Jacob Yoder could possibly have had in his buggy. Mr. Spiers had no inkling of the fantasy relationship his respectable young mentee had constructed in her disillusioned mind. It was in complete ignorance therefore that he divulged all there was to tell about Jacob and his young wife, Ruth Yoder. He told how Ruth's familye farmed in the neighboring Old Repton area and how Jacob and she had met during harvesting one year when Ruth was only sixteen. Maxine's illusion came apart at the seams as Mr. Spier's telling of the love story continued. By the time he started telling of the romantic proposal beside the picturesque Springfield Falls nearby, Maxine was fit to burst. Her unfounded anger at Jacob's perceived lies over the months and her resentment of Ruth who came in and ruined her future with the man she loved so completely, boiled over during Mr. Spier's enthusiastic relating of the Yoder fairytale. To say that the old man was taken aback at Maxine's explosive response would be a gross understatement at the very least. It was as if he was faced with a stranger in that moment, and certainly not the intelligent and very capable young lady he had hired so willingly to run his life's work when he no longer could. Maxine saw the shocked expression on the old man's face and excused herself before storming out of the shop.

She took a good while to calm herself, walking through the town's park, muttering incoherently to herself in an effort to align all she had just learnt about Jacob with the fantasy she had constructed for herself. By the time she turned to return to the pharmacy, she had convinced herself that Ruth was just a passing phase in the life of the man she loved. She could not be certain just yet what Jacob was using Ruth to achieve but she knew that it would all work out for the best in the end. All she had to do was keep her eye on the ball and the prize would follow. That had always worked for her in the past and it would work again to culminate in successfully making her Mrs. Jacob Yoder. When the mean blonde girls at school had taunted her when she failed to match their accomplishments in gym class in senior high, it had worked. She had set her goals on seeing them fail and they had. Every one of the five girls who had made a spectacle of her failure to achieve that day, had made one devastating mistake in their life which had led to the end of the figments they had built up in their imaginations of their perfect little existences. Her mother and father had lost all the friends they thought were important aspects of their lives. All the friends they had belittled their daughter in front of for all those years. Her parents had failed to impress the family members through their constant and unyielding condescension when she had made good without their assistance or even their input. She had broken all contact with them when she earned her scholarship. But only after making it widely known that she had achieved it all on her own and that her parents had played no role whatsoever in her success. Now everyone knew that Maxine Simpson was a self-made woman and that she did not need anyone. Maxine Simpson did not need to climb on anyone's shoulders to be important. She was important. She always had been. No one helped her and now she would never need anyone's help ever again. Now she had a man who loved her more than any woman could ever hope to be loved. She had Jacob Yoder, what more could she ask?

Jacob and Ruth Yoder

Ruth Miller was the only dochder of Noah and Mary Miller who farmed on the outskirts of Old Repton. She had a younger bruder by the name of Evan Miller who was destined to take over the farming when their parents were too old to farm any longer. That had become a joke in the area since Noah and Mary were only blessed with their two kinners very late in life. Many in the community did not think it likely that Mary would survive the first pregnancy being that she was already on the wrong side of fifty by then to even be bearing bopplis at all. When Gott blessed them very shortly after the birth of their first healthy boppli, Ruth, with yet another successful pregnancy and birth, the familye was ecstatic and complete. Then tragedy struck the farm when Noah was struck down walking back from visiting the neighbors at dusk on a September evening. Such was their bond that Mary followed not a month later, and the two were buried side by side in the community cemetery. So it was that their second-born and only son, Evan, was left alone to farm the familye's land.

But before tragedy befell the familye, they had lived happily together. Ruth had set the pace for her bruder and done well at school, but she dearly loved tending the farm animals and watching as the farming adapted to the seasonal changes year in and year out. She would ride with Jacob to the neighboring Amish community on the outskirts of the village of Volant when they were young enough to still live with their parents but old enough to no longer attend school. It was here that she first set eyes on Jacob Yoder while helping the farmers with their harvesting. It was the way of the Amish to band together to help with the annual harvests in their immediate and surrounding farmlands. Jacob was a little older than she, clean shaven and full of boyish charm and good humor. She watched as he cajoled the fellow Amish boys and girls of Volant whose parents had volunteered them to get the harvests in. He caught her watching him and his eyes sought her out throughout the day as he went about his business seeing to the bringing in of the crops. It was however many months before the two spoke to one another. That happened when the Yoders trundled into Old Repton to attend a wedding.

"So this is where you are to be found when you are not watching me across the market plain in Volant," Jacob teased Ruth during the festivities following the lengthy wedding ceremony. The two had eyed one another coyly all through the Bishop's sermon and the betrothed couple speaking their vows. Jacob could not wait to seek the girl out when they were free to mingle afterwards. He could also not help but marvel later that same day in the back of his parents' buggy on their way home after the wedding, that it only took one chance encounter to find the person who was destined to be in your life for all eternity. The one person chosen by Gott for you. What would happen, he wondered, if you missed your chance encounter and never got to find your one intended true love? He was certain that he would never have to worry about the answer to that question. He was certain too that he had already found the one Gott intended for him to spend his life beside; the one he was to start a familye of his own with one day when the time was right.

As it happened the time was right long before either of them anticipated it might be. Jacob's parents were taken at a young age not many years after the wedding they had attended in Old Repton. He was eighteen and had been baptized into the faith without a second thought. He was never one to wonder about Rumspringa and the allure of the Englischer life. Jacob Yoder knew where his destiny lay, and he had been farming it since he could first carry a shovel. He had buried his parents and he was now all alone in the world on the farm that was now his. His time had come to fulfill Gott's destiny for him, and Jacob knew that he was ready. Jacob Yoder knew also that the Millers would be happy to grant their permission for Ruth to marry at a young age since they were not expecting to live to see their kinners grow to the age that many parents might expect to see their children reach. So it was that Jacob spoke first with Noah Yoder and then with the Bishop of the Miller's Old Repton community to get permission to ask Ruth to be his wife. He had packed a small picnic basket and secreted it in a copse of trees beside the stream that ran through the Miller's farm. He invited Ruth to walk with him beside the stream and once there he retrieved the basket, lay a blanket out on the grassy banks beneath a shade tree and set out the treats. After they had tasted all the food and drinks he had thought to bring along, he got up onto one knee and asked Ruth to marry him. She was to be baptized that very week, and they were married after the traditional harvest season in October. Ruth could not wait to set up home with her husband on his farm which was not a far drive at all by buggy from the farm on which she had been raised.

"I don't think I have ever been as excited about the future as I am right now," Ruth had admitted to her bruder after her wedding.

"I am so happy for you, schweschder. Gott has blessed you with a gut mann and He will bless you with a wunderbaar life and a healthy familye," Evan had told her.

Gott had indeed done just that, and it was not long after the wedding that Ruth had the good fortune to tell her husband that she was expecting what he imagined would be the first of many bopplis. Although Jacob ventured into the larger town North of the village of Volant to get his asthma medication every month, Ruth had no inclination to go there. She had all she needed in the village of Volant and her own childhood area surrounding Old Repton. She did however accompany Jacob to the town once her belly indicated that they were to be blessed with a boppli all too soon. Jacob had started to show unease at leaving her at home alone while he was away from the farm later in her pregnancy and this was how she came to be beside him in the buggy as they trundled through the Main Street of the small neighboring town. She felt the unease of the situation before she even saw the woman responsible. With the visceral feeling came an inexplicable urge to look across the town's park as they drove past. Ruth saw the woman and thought how she who could not have been much older than her own bruder. She was dressed rather demurely for an Englischer, in a drab brown dress that hung midway between her knees and her ankles, made all the more odd by the dropped waistline. All in all she looked entirely incorrectly put together and out of place. But it was not her attire that bothered Ruth in passing. It was the look that the woman gave her, even in that briefest of moments, it was a haunting and disturbing glare. Ruth knew that any attempt to verbalize the bone chilling expression behind the stranger's eyes would only serve to make her herself seem somehow unhinged mentally. She put it down to her imagination spurred by the pregnancy and tried to forget it altogether. But it was much easier supposed than done.

Jacob and Ruth thanked Gott every night before they retired to bed for the easy pregnancy and asked His protection over them when the time came for the boppli to be born.

"Do you think it will be a boy or a girl?" Ruth asked Jacob as they climbed into bed together mere weeks before their boppli was due to be born into the world. She still could not believe that she was to be a mamm. Every day since she found out that they were expecting felt like Christmas and birthdays all wrapped up as one to Ruth. Jacob had been hard at work in his work shop fashioning a baby crib from wood for the baby who was already loved beyond measure by the expectant parents. Ruth had been working on a special baby quilt, helped by her mamm who was thrilled at the thought of being a grossmammi.

"I think that whatever boppli Gott has chosen for us will be just perfect, whether it is a boy or a girl," Jacob answered, looking proudly at his wife who seemed to grow before his eyes as her pregnancy developed.

Ruth laughed at his charming answer and kissed him good night before settling her head on her pillow.

When the time came for the boppli to be born, the sun was still high in the summer sky when Jacob ran out the kitchen door to call for the young boy who helped on the farm to fetch the midwife as quickly as he could. The midwife arrived in her buggy and issued instructions to the anxious Jacob as she rushed past him up the stairs as he was coming down. Not long after her arrival, Jacob was still boiling the large kettle of water on the wood stove as instructed when he heard the shrill and unmistakable cry of the boppli upstairs. He abandoned all sense of duty to the boiling of water and took the stairs three at a time, reaching the bedroom door as it was opened from the inside.

"You have a fine baby girl, Jacob Yoder. Your wife delivered her just fine and both mamm and boppli are in perfect health," the midwife congratulated the new daed as he pushed past her in the doorway to the bedroom. Jacob fell to his knees at the bedside and took both Ruth's hands in his as he thanked Gott for all His blessings.

"She is beautiful." Ruth beamed proudly as she moved the blanket from the swaddled boppli's face for Jacob to see.

"She had no choice but to be beautiful, given who her mamm is. I love you, Ruth," Jacob whispered against her hands, his eyes glued to his dochder's face.

Tempered by Fire

Five years later...

Ruth woke with a start with the strange woman's look foremost in her mind and sat bolt upright in the bed. It had been over five years since she had seen the woman's steely glare that day in the buggy, but the remembering of it never failed to cause her to shudder involuntarily. She could feel Jacob stir in the bed beside her. The night was dark and the ineffectual light that would have been provided by the sliver of a moon was covered by the cloud that hung low over the farm that night. She could feel her husband beside her more than she could hope to have seen him in the inky blackness of their bedroom. Instinctively her hand moved to her belly where she imagined she could feel the boppli move against her. But she knew that it was no more than her imagination since she was not yet even sure herself that she was pregnant with what might be their second boppli. As soon as she was certain, she would share the good news with Jacob. But for now they'd had too many false hopes for her to raise Jacob's hopes before she knew for sure. Ruth made to lie down again, and it was then that she caught the slight movement near the door of their room. Had there been even a hint of illumination that night, she would have put the stirring down to an insect. In the darkness however Ruth knew without a shadow of a doubt that someone was in their bedroom in the middle of the night. And that someone meant them harm. Her thoughts immediately went to little Becca asleep in her room next door. If there was someone in their bedroom, what were the chances that their dochder might already have been harmed?

Panic took a hold of her and she struggled against it to take her next breath. It was then that the woman stepped forward out of the shadow and made her presence known.

"You!" Ruth gasped, and the woman grinned malevolently.

"Yes. You always knew you would not get away with taking him from me. I knew you would be expecting me at some time," the woman answered.

Only then did Ruth smell the paraffin. "What have you done?" she breathed in disbelief.

"You don't deserve any of this. You stole my life and now you must lose it all. It does not belong to you. It never did. I will take it all away from you now. He was meant for me not for you. Never for you," the woman grimaced manically.

"Who?" Jacob groaned, woken from a deep sleep by the voices. He sat up in the bed and tried to make sense of what was happening in what was supposed to be the private sanctuary of a bedroom he shared with his wife.

"Oh, Jacob. Becca…. This woman is mad," Ruth sobbed, taking a hold of his arm and shielding herself with it as if his mere presence was all she needed to be safe.

"If I am mad, it is only because you stole from me," the woman suggested. "Light a lamp!" she instructed Jacob.

Jacob did as he was told and when the room was lit up he blustered, "Maxine? Maxine Simpson from the pharmacy?" Jacob's arm was still extended in front of his panic-stricken wife.

"Jacob, Becca?" Ruth reminded him.

Jacob started to get out of the bed to check on his dochder.

"It is too late for all that now," Maxine said evenly. "You made your choice and now we all have to suffer because of it," she continued.

"What do you mean it's too late?" Jacob showed the first signs of dread.

"Why did you choose her over me?" she asked with vehement disdain, gesturing towards the sobbing Ruth. "For years you have flaunted her before me. First her and then the child. What did I do to you to deserve that? I waited for you to come back to me. I waited!" Her voice became increasingly shrill as she seemed to lose control of her tenuous composure. "But you just kept me hanging. Every time you came into the pharmacy to see me, you tightened your hold on me, knowing all the time that you were never going to come back for me."

Jacob looked at Ruth whose eyes were full of confusion and questions. "But…" He tried to reason with a situation that was nothing but unreasonable in every possible way. "I never did go to see you. I was only there for my medication, not for you. Never for you." Jacob was openly apprehensive. He did not want to antagonize Maxine, who was very clearly not of sound mind in that moment. He also did not want to hurt his beloved Ruth by having her believe that he had any intentions with this mad woman.

How had this situation even come about, Jacob wondered to himself as he tried unsuccessfully to fathom what was happening in his haus in the middle of the night.

He knew before the events even got out of hand that there would never be any satisfactory answers to that question. At least not for him and Ruth. He prayed to Gott that his dochder was not hurt and that she would remain unscathed through it all, regardless of what happened that night in their haus.

"Pass me the lamp," Maxine commanded, nearing the bed. Jacob lifted the lit lamp and handed it across the bed and Ruth to Maxine. Maxine hardly took a hold of it before she loosened her grasp and the lamp hit the floor, catching the corner of the bed as it fell. The flames cascaded from the lamp onto the bed and across the floor. Ruth watched in horror as the quilt that covered her and Jacob caught fire. The quilt that her grossmammi had lovingly worked on especially for her before she was even born into this complicated world.

The last image Ruth and Jacob had before the fire

engulfed them in their bed was the demented eyes of the woman who had run the pharmacy by herself after Mr. Spiers had turned up mysteriously dead in his house all those years ago. The eyes looked out at them over a delighted smile.

Maxine watched as the love bed became a consuming fire and then she turned and walked to the child's bedroom. She stood in the doorway and waited until the sleeping form in the bed was illuminated by the fire that was spreading from the bedroom next door. She watched as the sleeping child began to cough before she had even woken up. She watched as the girl opened her eyes and she watched as terror rooted in the child's eyes as understanding bloomed in her immature little brain. Smoke began to obscure her view of the girl they called Becca who had now sat up in her bed and was calling, "Mamm! Daed! Help me." Calling to parents who could no longer be there for her as she had grown to expect.

Becca looked around the room in panic and her eyes fixed on Maxine's where she stood in the passageway outside her bedroom door. Maxine smiled at the child. The deranged arsonist felt the heat on her ankles and looked down at the floor. She cursed under her breath. She would not be able to see the child taken by the fire. It was no longer safe in the house. Maxine knew she had only one chance to get out or it would be too late for her. She also knew that she did not deserve to die here with these people who had stolen her life from her while they lived. Now it was her time to live because she had stolen her life back from them.

* * *

She ran down the burning stairs and out the kitchen door onto the porch. Embers were floating on the air all about the house and she thought she heard the cry of a child inside, but it may just have been the fire chasing the air from the burning rooms.

Maxine slept the sleep of the righteous that night, knowing that she had again been dynamic in accomplishing her destiny. Just after day break she drove the comfortable car that had been left to her along with Mr. Spier's entire estate to the outskirts of Volant, where the little Amish farms dotted the landscape. It would have been a peaceful and serene scene had it not been for the multitude of emergency vehicles with their flashing lights all busily coloring the gray remains of the Yoder homestead. Maxine parked her car at a distance and surveyed the commotion playing out before her. No one saw her. No one ever saw Maxine Simpson.

After the Yoder Haus Fire

Maxine fixed her hair and changed her clothes before making her way to the pharmacy. She unlocked it as she had every business day since Mr. Spiers had given her the keys and prepared the shop to receive customers. She took great delight in serenely lauding it over the beautiful women and girls of the greater district when they happened into her domain. She knew, and they would come to the realization sooner or later, that beauty faded way before the brain withered. They might be the beautiful ones now, but she would always be smarter than any of them. No one could take that away from her.

She had made a life for herself and earned her place in the sun here in the quiet, unassuming Pennsylvanian town tucked away among the smaller more rural villages. Sometimes she envied the married Amish women their simple life, but she knew now that because of Jacob Yoder's wrong choices, that life would never be hers. She was content with her lot for the moment.

* * *

She was satisfied that her life was to be no more than a pleasant platitude. Her thoughts were interrupted by the bell denoting a customer's entrance into the pharmacy.

"Why, good morning to you, Mrs. Stoltzfus. You are out and about early this fine morning. Can I be of some help?" greeted the uncharacteristically bubbly pharmacist from within her dispensary.

"Just picking up the anti-histamines for my husband, Miss Simpson. He'll be robbing the bee hives later today with the help of our sons, when the heat has worn off the day. One must always be prepared for any eventuality when dealing with Gott's little creatures, must one not?" the middle-aged wife of a local Amish farmer replied.

"Indeed, you are very right, Mrs. Stoltzfus. Will you be stocking my pharmacy shelves with your raw honey then, once you have the takings from today bottled?"

"It may be a little longer in coming this time around, Miss Simpson. What with all the mayhem around the poor Yoders' misfortune and all. We might all be called on to do our part in smoothing over the damage caused during the night over at their farm. A very unfortunate time for the community, it is. Sad to lose ones so young," Mrs. Stoltzfus clucked, shaking her head solemnly and looking down at her shoe respectfully.

"Lose ones so young?" Maxine echoed in the form of a question. "The Yoders? Whatever are you talking about now, Mrs. Stoltzfus? What misfortune?"

"Oh dear," the older lady gasped, her hand flying immediately to her mouth in distress. "You haven't heard? I guess you may just be a little too far afield for the communal word of mouth news out here. There was a terrible fire during the night. Jacob and Ruth Yoder's haus burnt to the ground. As far as anyone can tell, official-wise that is, a lamp must have fallen over in the upstairs bedrooms and taken the whole haus down within a very short time," Mrs. Stoltzfus explained, her eyes still fixed to the ground. "The neighbors only noticed after the fire had taken hold good and properly, though, and by the time they had formed a meaningful bucket line from the well to the inferno, it was too late to save the haus or the poor couple."

"The couple?" Maxine echoed again, "Jacob and Ruth, do you mean?"

"Jah," Mrs. Stoltzfus sighed resignedly. "Gott bless them in their passing. And their poor little dochder. Who knows what is to become of her?"

"Their dochder? She survived the fire?" Maxine blurted in surprise before she could help herself.

Mrs. Stoltzfus looked up at the startled Maxine, a look of surprise all her own blooming on her face. "Jah, thank Gott for His mercy, she is not harmed."

"But how would she have got out the burning haus if she was upstairs where the fire is believed to have started?" Maxine could not suppress her curiosity and the questions rose up in her chest, consuming her common sense.

"Miss Simpson, you seem disappointed that Gott chose to save the child. If it was not yet her time, Gott must have great plans for her. It is not for us to question His works, is it now? The child has not spoken since she was rescued outside the burning building. For this reason, no one quite knows the answers to the questions about how she escaped the flames. We are only too grateful that she did."

"Of course you are quite correct, Mrs. Stoltzfus, I am sorry if I seemed unsympathetic. I can assure you that that is very definitely not the case. It is a miracle, I am sure, that the girl did not die along with her unfortunate parents. But what is to become of her now?"

Mrs. Stoltzfus shrugged against the explanation. "Little Becca Yoder was taken to the children's hospital in the city by ambulance during the early hours of this morning. By all accounts, she is not injured."

"And when she is released from their care, what then?" Maxine pushed for an answer.

"I believe her uncle has been at her bedside most of the morning. He was roused from his bed in the farmlands around Old Repton and driven by the police to the hospital where he has kept constant vigil. Her grandparents were only buried very recently, and she has only Ruth's bruder left as familye now."

"Oh. An uncle. How fortunate for the girl," Maxine said but the expression in her eyes did not match the words from her mouth. "Thank you, Mrs. Stoltzfus, for keeping me up to date with this series of unfortunate events. Is it not wonderful that the child was saved the same fate as Jacob and Ruth? Will there be anything else for you today?" Maxine said as she handed the older lady her tablets.

"We should all be minders of our neighbors," Mrs. Stoltzfus shrugged. "Thank you for your help and I will be around with the bottles of honey just as soon as we have them ready for you. Gutentag, Miss Simpson."

Maxine rushed out from behind the dispensary counter to lock the door behind the receding Mrs. Stoltzfus. She flipped the sign around to show that the shop was now closed, locked the door, and made her exit out the rear door. She had her mobile phone on her. Any emergencies could either divert to the next town over or contact her by telephone. But then again, when last had these people known an emergency? Maxine drove onto the city and asked at reception after the Yoder child. She was given a room number, but she did not visit it. She lingered about the general area until she saw the Amish man leave the room and enter the men's room across the passageway. She took her chance then to slip into the room where the girl lay sedated in the bed that was especially designed for sick children. She did not pay the child much attention but lifted the chart from its holder at the foot of the bed and read the diagnosis and medication given. The child was in no danger of succumbing to any injuries. Miraculously she had escaped with none whatsoever. She was being treated for shock and smoke inhalation. How did Maxine allow this obstacle to her plans to occur? She slipped back out the room unseen before the Amish man even left the men's room. After all, no one ever saw Maxine Simpson.

Maxine sat in the hospital car park, drinking coffee from a paper cup and eating hospital vending machine sandwiches, and waiting for the Amish man to leave the hospital with the child. There was no good reason for the child to be kept hospitalized, therefore she should not have to wait too long for the two to materialize. Maxine knew from the chart that the doctors had found no medical reason for the child to be mute. Nonetheless the girl had apparently not spoken a word since the neighbors found her huddled beside the barn in the unfriendly night air, watching the burning house collapse with her parents inside. If the child spoke, she could very well expose Maxine as the villain who had changed her status from beloved dochder to orphaned child. Maxine could not permit that to happen. She could not be sure that the child did not somehow know her. She could think of no reason why the child should know who she was, but there was no good reason to leave ends untied unnecessarily. Who would miss an orphaned girl? Would it not be seen as a blessing that she was sent to join her dead parents wherever it was that the believers imagined the dead went when life was done with them?

Maxine had finished one more disappointing coffee than she had hoped to have to endure before the Amish uncle emerged from the hospital doorway. Ahead of him was a hospital orderly, pushing a child-sized wheelchair in which sat a deflated form of a girl. Maxine sat up straighter in her seat and watched as the unlikely trio crisscrossed the busy parking lot to a taxi waiting in the parking area designated for transportation of that nature. The orderly helped the girl into the back seat while the man took his place beside her. The taxi started up just as soon as the orderly had removed himself and the wheelchair from its way, and it edged slowly out the parking lot. Maxine fired up her car's engine and followed the taxi at a discreet distance through the city and out into the countryside. She thought to herself how lucky it was that she had filled the fuel tank earlier that week. She had no cause to use the car much in her daily life. She could and did walk to the pharmacy on most mornings, unless she had plans to leave the town for any reason during any given day. Which did not happen very often at all. She followed the taxi for many miles until it bypassed the small village of Old Repton and took a gravel road to the farmlands. Maxine knew better than to follow along this route, which would only arouse suspicion with anyone who spotted an unknown vehicle on the farm roads normally traveled only by Amish horse drawn buggies. She parked on a high point overlooking the general area in which the taxi had traveled and was rewarded with a view of it turning into the yard of a well-maintained Amish homestead. The Amish man alighted and went around to the other side of the taxi to extract the girl from the back seat. He paid the taxi, which reversed without further ado out the yard and back the way it had come. Maxine watched as the man carried the girl up the stairs and onto the porch and then unlocked the door to the house. He must live alone, she thought to herself, and then she remembered Mrs. Stoltzfus mentioning that the girl's grandparents had only recently passed away. His clean-shaven face was a telltale sign that the Amish uncle was unmarried, so of course he would be living alone. That would make it easier for Maxine to carry out what needed to be done next. She started the engine and maneuvered her car back onto the quiet country road. Maxine watched as the peaceful countryside of Old Repton receded in her rearview mirror and she returned to her home and her life. No one noticed the car. No one saw Maxine Simpson arrive or leave the area. No one had ever seen Maxine Simpson, after all.

Maxine had always known what would happen next, because she had these plans for her life. Fate was not her friend. She would mark her own path. Maxine Simpson had only ever had herself to rely on. But when she got back to her house, furnished by the dead pharmacist, and resumed her work in the prosperous little pharmacy which had been established by a dead man, she found no satisfaction. Why was life turning on her? She had alleviated all the obstacles to her mission, had she not? Where was her happiness, then? Why did she have no feelings of contentment and joy? Where had she gone wrong?

Maxine had all these questions coursing through her mind when the bell tingled on the door and a young couple clearly in love entered the pharmacy, hand in hand. The young woman perused the suntan lotions while the man selected a package and carried it over to the till to pay. Maxine did not know why it angered her to see what the man was buying, but it did. She did not like that young lovers flaunted their relationships so openly in front of her when she had lost the love of her life in that awful house fire so recently. She slammed her fist on the counter and the young man stepped back in shock.

"Get out!" Maxine screeched at the top of her voice. "Get out right now, both of you! You are despicable and

God sees what you are doing. Don't think that your secrets are secret. They are not. They never were and they never will be. People know what you are and what you do. Get out of my shop!"

By then she had rounded the counter and was pushing the surprised woman towards the door. The man got to the door first and opened it, reaching back to grasp his girlfriend, who he pushed out the door ahead of him. Maxine closed the door behind them and glared at them as they stumbled to their car, looking over their shoulders in shock at the mad woman standing at the glass doors. Maxine went into the back room and removed the bobby pins from her hair. She brushed her hair out and it fell in pathetic oily strips down her shoulders. She had just started pinning her hair up into a bun at the back of her head when the bell tingled out front. She called out in a mumbled voice around the bobby pin between her lips that she would be right out. But the person did not wait and she saw the man as he poked his head around the doorway into her private back room. Another followed immediately behind him and the first man stepped boldly into her space. Before she knew what was happening, she felt the hypodermic needle in her upper arm. The world suddenly seemed a better place as the faces of the two men she had seen as invaders of her sanctuary swirled before her into a kaleidoscope of facial features. Then the comforting blackness swallowed her and she was falling through a cloud of loving acceptance.

The Prognosis

"Your daughter is a very disturbed young woman, Mr. and Mrs. Simpson. I am quite sure that she will never cope with life outside these walls," the attending psychiatrist, Doctor Peter Swayles, tapped on the folder marked MAXINE MAY SIMPSON in bold and accusing letters as he leaned on his oversized wooden desk with the obligatory leather inset.

"But surely there is something you can do for her that will make her better again," Margery Simpson retaliated in what could have been taken as an accusatory tone. "How in blazes does a perfectly intelligent woman who finished top of her class in half the time as the other students get labeled committable?" She exaggerated the last word by thumping both hands heavily on the desk that the doctor was thankful stood quite firmly between him and her.

"We will have to work with her for a lot longer to answer all those questions, but for the time being we do know that she suffers from more than a handful of syndromes classified in the *Diagnostic and Statistical Manual of Mental Disorders*. Psychologically she is unfit to contribute effectively to society. Working with her so far has unveiled her proclivity to attachment disorders. She is abnormally possessive in her relationships," the doctor explained.

"How can you even suggest that?" Maxine's father demanded.

"The term often used for this is obsessive love disorder. Symptoms may include an overwhelming attraction to one person accompanied with obsessive thoughts about the person. We believe from speaking with the townspeople after your daughter's outburst in her pharmacy that she may have shown these tendencies towards a Jacob Yoder, an Amish man who farmed nearby. According to sources, Jacob's wife, Ruth, had mentioned her unease about your daughter's intentions towards her. Although Ruth Yoder and your daughter never actually met, to the best of anyone's knowledge, Ruth was known to be terrified by the manner in which your daughter looked at her. Your daughter's possessive thoughts and actions and extreme jealousy over Jacob Yoder's interpersonal interactions with his wife were somewhat alarming."

"But why does this Amish man and his wife have anything to do with Maxine?" Margery asked, throwing her husband an impatient look.

"Mr. and Mrs. Simpson, it is believed your daughter may have been involved with the burning down of the house in which Jacob and Ruth were burnt alive."

The doctor was impressed that Mrs. Simpson had

the good grace to gasp at this revelation. "Sufferers of obsessive love disorder may also not take rejection well at all. In the case that is becoming apparent with your daughter and her involvement with Jacob Yoder, it seems that she believed that she and he had a relationship. When it came to her attention well after she had formed an unhealthy compulsive obsession with Jacob that he was happily married, her symptoms escalated. This is normal in the matter of this abnormal disorder. The perceived rejection was too much for your daughter. When she constantly was faced with evidence of his love for another, once again exacerbated by Ruth falling pregnant and producing a daughter as a testimony of their love, Maxine's mental capacity was not strong such that she could handle it effectively."

"Why did we not see this before? Surely if our perfectly intelligent daughter had a mental problem, we would have noticed as much?" Mark Simpson argued, reassuringly patting his wife's hand.

"I can mention some telltale signs that are often overlooked as normal or perhaps somewhat eccentric. Did she show a constant need for reassurance, difficulty forming or maintaining friendships, and/or a lack of contact with family members?" the doctor enquired.

His answer came in the form of the body language displayed by the increasingly distraught parents seated before him. Margery dropped her shoulders and wept into her hands. Mark folded his head into his neck and looked towards the ceiling, closing his eyes as if to block out the intolerable disclosure.

* * *

The doctor closed the file marked MAXINE MAY SIMPSON and dropped it irreverently into his desk drawer.

Doctor Peter Swayles, MD, accompanied the resigned parents out of his consulting room and into the general passageways of the mental asylum. Their daughter would spend her time here leading up to the trial in which she would be tried for arson and murder. Now they would know why, and no longer try to make excuses for her. The doctor shook hands with Mark Simpson and then lightly took Margery's hand before they turned and made their way to their waiting car. The doctor watched as Mark opened the door for his wife and closed it again when she was securely seated in the passenger seat. He continued to watch as Mark walked around the car, opened the driver's door, and took his place behind the steering wheel, closing the door firmly before he started up the engine. No one saw Maxine watching them, too, from the third-floor window, where she had to peer through the heavily barred windows to see her parents ultimately abandoning her yet again.

As fate would have it, to which of course Maxine rendered no part, Maxine was found unfit to stand trial. She was therefore remanded to institutionalization in the asylum for mentally disturbed patients. After two years of being a prisoner among the insane people, Maxine was growing bored with the games she had been playing with the doctors, psychiatrist, and the array of medical professionals who were set upon her constantly. She was reviewed continuously and it was during one such one-on-one session with Doctor Peter Swayles, MD, that she secreted a pertinent page of his newspaper into her dress. Later that night she read with great interest the column of one Holly Miller, erstwhile journalist and now the wife of a Pennsylvanian man who had taken on caring for his orphaned niece some two years back. *So the little beggar has made a new life for herself with a new mommy and daddy, and here I am stuck with a building full of loonies living no life at all*, she thought to herself after reading the article. Plans were immediately underway to rectify that.

Maxine seemed to be coping better with life inside than she had seemed to be during her latter time as a woman of liberty in the Pennsylvanian countryside. As such she was eventually given more freedom of movement within the grounds of the asylum. She very cleverly manipulated her position until that fateful day when she very casually slipped out of the yard along with the day's visitors. In no time at all Maxine was on a train bound for Pennsylvania. She knew exactly where she was heading and she knew exactly what is was she would have to do once she was there. That girl had meant to die with her life-destroying parents in that fire when she was younger. The girl they called Becca was not intended to live. Only a fortnight after her escape, she was watching the little girl in the streets of Old Repton as she went about her uninterrupted life with her baby sister and the couple she now regarded as Mamm and Daed.

Maxine became obsessed with Becca. She watched her almost constantly and when she did not have her in her sights, she had her in her dreams and in her fantasies. She had convinced herself that Becca was her only remaining obstacle to the life she was intended to live. Evan Miller had been a tool in her survival, the man who had given her the life that Maxine was convinced was standing in the way of her very happiness. The child alive robbed her of her deserved joy. She had to die as destiny had intended all those years earlier. Destiny was not to be detoured.

Flames

On the night after Becca and Evan had reported the mystery woman to the local police...

After Becca and Evan returned from town, Evan stayed at the haus. He quietly worked around the yard, chopping wood they didn't need, pulling weeds that didn't need pulling...anything he could find to keep his hands busy and his mind off the fact that out there was a woman who wanted to cause him and his familye harm. It bothered him, and his anger and irritation were palpable.

Holly did her best to keep Becca's mind occupied throughout the day, and he could see the relief on her face when Becca finally headed to her bed for the night. The only familye member seemingly unaffected by all that was happening on the farm was Hope. She was a happy boppli and learning to talk. Her constant chatter was the only bright spot in everyone's day.

"Is Becca sleeping?" Evan asked as Holly joined him in the living area.

Holly stopped in the doorway and turned around. "I was putting Hope to bed. I didn't hear her in her room. Do you think I should go check on her?"

Evan pushed up from his chair and nodded. "She seemed calm, but I worry that today's events might be the cause of her nightmares returning."

"I shall leave her bedroom door open a bit." Holly gave him a smile and walked back up the stairs. She turned the handle on Becca's bedroom door and pushed it open a crack, frowning ever so slightly when she found the room to be completely dark. Becca almost always fell asleep with the lantern lit and either Evan or Holly would step in and douse it before going to bed themselves.

"Becca?" Holly whispered, not wanting to frighten the little girl by her arrival. When she got no response, she pushed the door open further and used her own lantern to illuminate the room. She quickly lit the lantern placed on Becca's side table and then she realized that the little girl wasn't in her bed. She raised her voice a bit. "Becca? Dochder, come out from your hiding place."

Holly set the lantern down on the side table and bent to look beneath the bed. Aside from a small standing wardrobe and dresser, the only other items in the room were a trunk in the corner that held a few salvaged items from Jacob and Ruth Yoder's haus. Becca's parents.

"Becca?" Holly called out again, not finding her beneath the bed. Growing alarmed, she stepped to the doorway and called for Evan, not caring if she woke Hope. "Evan! Evan!"

He appeared at the bottom of the stairs. "What is it?"

Holly shook her head, dread filling her heart. "She's not in her bed."

"Becca?" Evan asked, taking the stairs two at a time. Hope's plaintive cry announced that she was now also awake again.

Holly walked down the hall. "I'll get Hope. Where would Becca have gone?"

"She came up the stairs to go to bed. She didn't come back down."

Holly grabbed Evan and they both searched the other rooms upstairs and then those downstairs. No sign of Becca was to be found. Holly was growing panicked. "We have to find her."

Evan nodded. "We will. Maybe she went outside…"

Holly shook her head. "She was afraid to go out in the sunlight, she wouldn't go outside in the dark. Not by herself." She looked at Evan in dawning horror. "You don't think…?"

Evan placed an arm around her shoulders. "Don't allow those negative thoughts to take root. We'll find her."

"I'm going to take Hope over to the Schoenfelds'."

"That is gut idea," Evan told her. "I'll get my boots on."

Holly grabbed the small quilted bag that contained a change of clothing for Hope and some fresh diapers and dashed for the front door. Hope seemed excited about this change to her routine and was babbling happily as

Holly made her way across the yard that separated the two farms. The Schoenfelds were an older Mennonite couple who had moved to Old Repton a few years back.

They mostly kept to themselves but had proven to be gut neighbors in the past. Holly hoped she wouldn't be inconveniencing them too much by her arrival. Mr. Schoenfeld met her at the door. "Holly? Child, what are you and that precious baby doing out at this time of night?"

"Becca has gone missing and we need to find her. Could I impose upon you and your wife to watch Hope for me so that I can help Evan search?"

"Certainly. Come in…"

Holly shook her head. "I need to get back. Denke. I'll be back as soon as we find her."

"Take your time. I'll put her to bed with our grand-daughter for the night. She arrived today for a short visit. She's about the same age as your Becca. You don't worry about Hope, you just go find that little girl of yours."

Holly nodded. "We will." She turned and that's when she saw the slight glow rising from the side of their haus. A plume of smoke was rising along with the glow, and Holly took off running, yelling for Evan as she neared the front porch. He stepped out and she waved towards the side of the haus. "The barn! It's on fire!"

Evan bounded down the stairs and they rushed around the corner of the haus to see the left side of the barn engulfed in flames. Evan threw the doors open and what he and Holly saw inside made his insides clench in renewed anger. A strange woman, resembling the description Becca had given of the woman, was dragging Becca by her hair and her collar towards the far side of the barn.

"Stop struggling, you little brat!" the woman screamed at her.

Evan put an arm out and held Holly back when she tried to rush to Becca's aid. "Wait! Let me talk to her."

He stepped inside the burning barn, praying that he would be able to get the woman to let Becca go before they were all trapped by the fire. "Stop!"

The woman turned, her face contorted in pure rage. "Stay back!"

"The barn is on fire. You need to let Becca go and get out of here."

"No! She was supposed to die with her parents and I'm going to fix that tonight."

"Her parents' death was an accident…" Evan began, stopping when reality set in. "It wasn't an accident, was it?"

The woman shook her head. "Of course not."

"Who are you? Did you know Ruth and Jacob?" Evan kept her talking, because while she was talking she was no longer dragging Becca further into the burning structure.

"I lived next door to them for years. My name is Maxine Simpson and this brat's dad was once mine."

Evan raised a brow at her insinuation. Jacob had been unfaithful to Ruth? Never! He had known his bruder-in-law and there was no way Jacob Yoder had cheated on his wife. He kept these thoughts to himself, allowing the woman to continue speaking.

"He wouldn't leave that cow he married. He should have been mine, but he stayed with her. And then this brat came along and I knew I would never get him back."

"So you killed them?" Evan asked, slowly making his way ever closer to the woman. He could feel Holly behind him and only hoped he would be able to save them all.

"I got my revenge. They were so trusting. Setting their house on fire was child's play."

Holly touched his back and murmured near his ears. "We need to get Becca away from her. The fire is spreading quickly."

Evan nodded and kept his voice calm, but inside he was churning with anxiety. "Maxine, I'm sure Jacob never meant to hurt you."

Maxine was upset and growing ever more agitated. Evan felt Holly slip to his side, using a pile of hay to hide her movements. He moved in the opposite direction, keeping Maxine's attention focused on him. She had let go of her hold on Becca's hair and now only loosely held the back of her nightgown in one hand.

"Maxine, did you hurt the horses and the chickens? My crops?"

"You helped her," Maxine released Becca as she gestured towards her with both hands. "You had to pay for helping her."

The moment Becca felt that the woman had released her nightdress, she bolted for the opposite side of the barn where Holly was waiting to catch her. The abrupt movement startled Maxine and Evan wasted no time in lunging at her, tackling her to the ground, face down so that she couldn't effectively fight back.

He glanced to his right and saw that Holly had Becca safely in her arms. A crack overhead let him know with no uncertainty that the fire had spread to the high cross-beam. The entire barn was in danger of collapsing and they needed to get to safety. Now!

"Go! Get out of the barn!" he yelled to Holly. He struggled to drag the woman to her feet, the necessity of reaching the safety of the yard giving him added strength and determination. Holly carried Becca from the burning structure and he struggled to follow them, coughing as smoke and heat burned his lungs and his eyes. Maxine was talking incoherently now, her anger replaced by a behavior that more than suggested certain insanity.

"We have to get out of here. Now!" She struggled against him, trying to run back into the fire, but Evan was stronger than she was. He part dragged and part carried her out of the burning structure only moments before the left side collapsed in on itself and the remaining structure burst into flames. They'd made it out alive, and now Evan wanted his questions answered.

Familye

A small crowd had started to gather, the Schoenfelds had seen the smoke and raised the alarm. All their neighbors had rushed to their aid with buckets and shovels. They were preparing to form a bucket line from the water pump in the yard to the barn, but Evan shook his head when he heard the sound of a fire truck coming up the long lane.

"Leave the firefighters to get on with their job."

Everyone stood back as the red truck turned into the yard. Within moments water was streaming from their yellow hoses, aimed at quelling the flames before the rest of the structure collapsed. Behind them several police cars followed and Evan gratefully relinquished Maxine to their expert hands.

Holly came to him then, lifting Becca into his waiting arms. "Becca!"

"Daed!"

"She's okay. She said Maxine dragged her out the window."

The window under discussion was no less than

twenty feet off the ground. "It's a wonder they didn't fall and hurt themselves."

"I was scared. She was the woman in my room the night the haus burned down."

"You're positive it was her?" Holly asked softly.

Becca nodded. "I'm sure. I remember her eyes."

"Well, she can't hurt you anymore now."

Holly reached for Becca when the police officer who had taken their statement earlier that day walked up. "Folks, I wish we could have gotten here sooner. That's one crazy lady."

Evan nodded. "You know who she is?"

"Yes, unfortunately. She's been staying in the next town over and registered under her real name. Maxine Simpson."

"She was a neighbor of my late schweschder and her husband. She admitted to starting the fire that burned their haus down. She seems to think that she and Jacob, my bruder-in-law, had some sort of relationship."

"I know all about that," the officer commented. "I had just finished reading her case worker's notes when I heard the call for a firetruck come over the radio. I recognized the address and rushed out here."

"Case worker?" Evan asked, trying to find answers for his questions.

"The woman is crazier than a loon. It seems that she took a liking to Jacob Yoder and envisioned a life together with him. When he married your sister, she grew unbearably jealous and decided to kill them all. She lives in a fantasy world most of the time and doesn't seem to have any remorse about killing them. She thought Becca had died in the fire as well."

Evan shook his head. "I still don't understand...who exactly is this woman?"

"Maxine Simpson is twenty-nine and about as delusional as they come. She grew up as a neighbor of Jacob. She was a pharmacist at the local drugstore and developed a possessive love for him. A love that wasn't returned. She reports being very hurt and angry because he continued to ignore her. She envied Ruth's position in his life and hated her for it."

"But why would she kill Jacob if she thought she loved him?"

The officer shrugged his shoulders. "I'm not even going to try to say I understand a mind like hers. I guess she figured if she couldn't have him, no one could. Anyway, she grew depressed after the fire and her family had her committed to a state mental institution for her own protection. They were afraid she might try to take her own life."

Evan turned and watched as Maxine was pushed into the back of a police car. "How did she get out?"

"She read an article your wife wrote in which she mentioned you taking Becca in to live with you after the fire. It was assumed that she didn't realize Becca had survived and it became her sole focus in life...to finish the job she started years earlier."

"She convinced them to let her out?" Evan questioned.

"No, she escaped. It took her a couple of years to accomplish the task, and multiple attempts, but she found a way out a few weeks back. She came here looking for Becca and found you. I spoke to her case worker and he thinks she would have transferred some of her anger to you because you helped Becca by taking her in. You became the enemy and she set out to destroy you and everything you hold dear. Your farm. Your animals. Your familye. She wouldn't have stopped until she'd killed you all."

Evan was stunned that any one person could show such violence to other living beings and hold such a level of hatred inside them. "So what happens now?"

The officer made a face. "There's no way she'll be able to stand trial. She's crazy. They'll put her into another facility, this time one for the criminally insane and make sure she can't get out again. Her family is waiting for her and will make sure she gets whatever help is available to her. She'll never be right, but maybe they can eventually get her to the point where she realizes what she's done is wrong."

The officer turned and looked at the barn, which had not been salvageable. "I'm going to take some pictures for my report and then I'll need to get a statement from your wife and daughter."

Evan nodded. "Come up to the haus when you're ready. I'll let Holly know." He joined Holly and Becca and then saw the Schoenfelds walking across the yard with Hope in their arms. He took her from them. "Denke for helping my familye."

"No thanks are needed, Evan. You found Becca, I see?"

"Jah. She's had a fright, but she is okay."

Holly hugged Becca close. "We're going up to the haus to make some kaffe for the workers. Would you like to join us?"

The older couple shook their heads. "No, it's way

past our bedtime, we just wanted to make sure everything was okay. Hope was an angel."

"Denke again for caring for her."

"Anytime. You take care of your familye tonight. Tomorrow is a new day and we'll be happy to help you start rebuilding in any way you need."

Holly took the girls up to the haus while Evan thanked his friends and neighbors for coming out and offering their assistance. Everyone expressed their desire to help the Millers rebuild the farm, and when Evan finally came to the kitchen door, his spirits were somewhat lifted and he paused for a moment to give Gott thanks.

"Gott, I don't understand why things happen the way they do, but I thank You that Becca is safe and unharmed. Thank You for Your hedge of protection this night and for gut friends and neighbors who stick together during times of great need. I'm sorry for my anger and I ask that You would help me forgive the woman who caused all of this.

"I ask that she would find the help that she needs to calm her mind and her irrational actions...please bring peace to her familye as well.

"Finally, thank You for my familye. For Becca and the joy that she brings to our lives. For Hope and the promise of a future and a brighter day she brought into Holly's and my life. And for Holly. *Denke, Gott!* She's the best thing that has ever happened to me and I ask that You would just bless her as she has been a blessing to me."

His prayer finished, he stepped inside the haus where he was surrounded by people who loved him and who meant more to him than any animal, structure, or crop. His familye.

Conversation with Gott

❧

The Miller Farm on the day following the barn fire...

Holly looked out the kitchen window as the sound of another buggy arriving drew her attention. This was how the day had been since early that morning after the firetrucks and police cars had left the farm, and the smoldering remains of the barn fire had been declared safe to leave unattended by the fire chief.

Evan had insisted on staying awake and had only returned to the haus for a few hours' sleep before the community started descending upon them. A steady stream of visitors to the farm had ensued, with gifts of food, promises of help rebuilding the barn, and offers for Evan and his workers to harvest produce from several nearby farms to fill their grocery orders.

Holly wasn't surprised by the offers, but nevertheless, she was reminded again of how differently the Amish dealt with crisis, in comparison to the Englisch way of doing things. Tragedy brought the Amish together and made them stronger.

The next few weeks were very stressful for Holly and Evan. School was still in session, and Holly was grateful that Becca had a short reprieve away from the farm each day. She was back to being a happy little girl, her nightmares having disappeared once again.

The police officer she'd spoken to had come to the farm three days after the incident with Maxine in the barn and explained that she was several states away and would be spending the rest of her life securely incarcerated. Her familye had written a note to Evan and Holly, asking them to forgive their daughter for her actions. The police officer had scoffed at the idea, but Evan had simply nodded and told him he was working on it.

Holly had secretly smiled at the shocked look on the mann's face. In the Englisch world, people didn't easily forgive or forget minor infractions. Trying to destroy and kill someone would never garner forgiveness in that world. But in the Amish world, Gott was their main focus and He required them to forgive those who wronged them. Without the ability to forgive, how could they truly understand the sacrifices that Gott had made for them?

Hope was growing even faster, it seemed, and Holly had her work cut out for her trying to keep the little girl out of the workmen's way. She always seemed to wander towards the pile of lumber that had been delivered by a nearby lumberyard two days after the fire. Even though it was getting close to harvest time for most in their small community, one or two menner were always on hand to volunteer their time on the farm to help rebuild the barn.

Several members of a neighboring Community had heard about Evan's troubles and had delivered four horses. Evan had insisted on paying for the animals, but his funds had been declined and they'd only requested payment in the form of farm produce. Evan had gladly loaded the back of their wagon with an abundant supply of apples, corn, and a variety of squash that were already ripened, with the promise of more deliveries in the future.

Holly smiled at the newcomers as they entered the kitchen. "Gutentag."

"Gutentag."

The three women, Dawn, Anna, and Abby, had all been friends of her mamm in her younger days. Since coming to live amongst the Amish, Holly had gotten to know the three women and she treasured their friendship.

"We saw Evan in the yard and he said our timing was perfect. They are raising the barn tomorrow?"

Holly nodded. "Jah. Everyone will be arriving before the sun's even up."

"Well, we came to help. What's first on the list? Breads or pies?" Dawn asked.

Holly grinned. "Both, now that I have so much help."

Anna laughed and tied an apron around her waist. "Where's Hope?"

Holly pointed to her side and the three women peeked over the kitchen work table to see the toddler sitting on the floor with a stack of measuring cups spread out before her. "She likes to help in the kitchen and stacking up the cups seems to be her favorite activity lately."

Dawn giggled. "My nephew likes to bang on the metal bowls with the wooden spoons. Count yourself lucky her chosen activity is a quiet one."

Holly nodded and smiled. She did count herself lucky and very blessed. Gott had provided her with a familye full of grandparents, aunts and uncles, and a community that had welcomed her with open arms once they got to know her. She'd met an honorable mann who loved her, second only to his love for Gott, and together they were raising two very precious little girls.

She grabbed a box of apples from the counter and the women started peeling and coring them, in preparation for the numerous pies that would be needed to feed the people who would be joining them tomorrow. Their own wives would bring a selection of food to be shared, but Holly was determined to make sure there was plenty of food and drink regardless. These people were going to be sacrificing their own chores and duties to help her husband out, and she wanted to make sure they all knew how grateful she and Evan were for their help.

"So Becca is doing okay now?" Dawn asked.

Holly nodded. "She said she's not had any more nightmares, but I certainly have. I keep seeing that woman holding her inside the burning barn."

Abby was closest to her and she wrapped an arm around her shoulders. "You can't dwell on that. Becca is fine and everyone made it out of the fire."

Holly tried to smile. "I know that, but I still can't help remembering the fear I felt."

"You need to give it over to Gott. With everything else that's been going on, I'm not surprised you're having trouble forgetting. Why don't you go lie down for a bit and let us get the pies ready for the oven?"

Holly shook her head. "Nee, I can't rest…"

"Why not? You weren't expecting our help today and here we are. Take Hope upstairs and have a nap with her. You have dark circles beneath your eyes and it's obvious you've been doing too much."

Holly looked at her friends and then nodded. "I haven't slept well. There always seems to be something else that needs doing."

"Then consider us your helpers today. Go take a nap and spend a few moments with Gott. You'll feel better afterwards."

Holly lifted Hope into her arms, took one more look at her friends and the bowls of apples, before she climbed the stairs to the bedroom she shared with Evan. Hope was ready for a nap, and a chance to have one with her mamm's arm wrapped around her was a pleasant and welcome surprise. Within moments the little girl was sound asleep, leaving Holly alone with her thoughts and Gott.

"I don't even know where to begin. Gott, thank You for keeping everyone safe. Denke. Continue to help Becca overcome the past. Please watch over Evan and give him strength to continue working these long hours. Keep him safe as well."

She paused for a moment, allowing her own thoughts and feelings about Maxine to surface. She was angry at the woman and the damage she'd done to her familye. She knew that Evan was working on forgiving her, but that was where Holly was really struggling.

She closed her eyes and continued her conversation with Gott.

"Help me find it within my heart to forgive Maxine for her actions. I'm happy she's getting some professional help, but I'm so angry with her. Gott, please help me find a place of peace. Allow me to look forward and to quit dwelling on what might have happened and didn't.

"I know You have great things in store for Evan and me, and I don't want an ungrateful spirit or unforgiveness to keep Your blessings from being poured out on us. I trust You and I put my faith in Your ability to carry me through this difficult time, just like You have in the past.

"I give You my anger and my anxiety right now. I trust that You only have gut planned for me and I accept that everything is working to accomplish Your plan. Denke, Gott for Your patience and I pray that I can fix my mind on things that would please You."

She started thinking about all the blessings in her life as she drifted off to sleep. She woke an hour later feeling more at peace and rested than she had since Becca had first mentioned her nightmares having returned. After washing her face and changing Hope's diaper, she returned to the kitchen and her friends. The alluring aroma of freshly baked pies lingered in the air and she rejoiced in the knowledge that everything was going to be okay. Gott was in control and she knew that to be true. Her strength came from the Lord and from this day forward, she was going to place her trust and her future in His hands. The past couldn't be changed and didn't deserve her energy; that belonged to the present day and the future.

Epilogue

One month later...

Holly sat on the front porch, the smell of Fall was in the air. The leaves on the trees were beginning to turn golden yellow and orange, and the final fields of corn would be harvested in just a few days. She watched as Becca and Hope walked around the yard with Becca naming the various flowers and pointing out interesting things to her schweschder. Becca's beloved cat was leading the way, and Holly smiled as snippets of the two girls' conversation reached her ears.

"Now Hope, that is a butterfly. He didn't always look like that, though. He was a green caterpillar who spent his time crawling across the leaves, eating his way along until he was fat and plump and ready to take a long nap."

Hope shook her head. "Don't want a nap!"

Becca giggled. "Not you, silly. The caterpillar. He would have had to take a nap so that he could grow into the butterfly."

Hope looked at her schweschder, appearing to understand, but Holly highly doubted Hope even knew what a caterpillar was. She would just have to wait until next Spring to see one for herself. The time for caterpillars was long gone now.

"Holly!" Evan called from the other side of the yard.

She waved at her husband and joined him as he brought the buggy to a stop and hopped out, a wide smile on his face. "What has you smiling so widely?"

"Gott is so good to us!" Evan told her, sweeping her up by the waist and spinning her around.

Holly laughed and held on to his shoulders for balance when he set her back down. "Tell me what has happened."

"We've been asked to provide produce to three more grocery stores!"

"Three more?" Holly asked with a smile. "And where are you going to grow this produce?"

"That's what has me so happy. I would have to purchase more land and hire more workers, but several of our neighbors approached me and want to partner with us. They've offered their fields and fruit trees and will help provide the additional produce needed to meet the stores' demands."

"Wunderbaar! That is great news!"

"Isn't it? We need to celebrate!"

"How do you propose we do that, husband?" Holly asked on a giggle. He was like a kid again and she loved seeing him carefree like this once more. Rebuilding the farm from scratch had been difficult, but four weeks later and many hours of volunteer labor from their community had set it back to rights.

Evan had let go of his anger and harsh feelings towards Maxine, choosing instead to offer her his forgiveness, even though it probably didn't mean anything to the mentally ill woman. His love for his familye had kept him focused on the days ahead, and Holly loved seeing him back to his happy and peaceful self.

"How about we go fishing?" he suggested with an infectious grin.

"Fishing?"

"Sure. Hope has never caught a fish…"

"She's only three. I don't think she's going to catch one today either," Holly told him with a grin.

"Fine. I'll catch the fish and she can watch. Becca likes to fish."

Holly laughed. "Becca likes anything that involves being in the outdoors. I'll go pack us a lunch while you find the fishing poles… Wait! The poles were in the barn…"

Evan nodded and then smiled. "I borrowed some from Herr Schoenfeld before coming home. They're already in the buggy."

Holly shook her head at him as he jogged over to join the girls who were still walking around the flower beds. She headed indoors to make sandwiches that they would eat for lunch. She added some apples, a loaf of the bread she'd baked earlier that morning, and some fresh butter. Several jars of fresh water made it into the basket as well as a jar of milk for the girls to share.

She grabbed a quilt off the back of the couch, and the

book she had been reading to Becca and Hope over the last several weeks. It was a story she'd read many times, about a young boy who'd found himself orphaned and alone who had risen above countless obstacles to become a mann of great influence and success.

"Ready to go?" Evan called from the kitchen door.

Holly nodded and pointed towards the basket she had set on the counter. "Lunch is packed."

"Gut! Let's go catch a fish. Or two."

The small familye set off, waving to their neighbors as they passed them along the road. The sun was shining overhead, the weather was just right, not too warm and not cold enough to warrant a jacket. The new barn's roof shone against the field, its shiny new tin much nicer than the shingled roof of the old barn.

The fields were vibrant with colors and produce, giving testimony to the fact that tragedy could come and go, but the circle of life remained unstaunched. Gott's marvelous creations were all around them, and while mann could try to destroy what He had created, mann would only succeed for a Season.

Gott had brought this little familye together, and even though a deranged woman had tried to destroy them, Gott had protected them through everything and brought them through it. Together.

Holly smiled at Evan over the top of the girls' heads, her love for him echoed in his own eyes. Her relationship with Evan had been tested almost since the beginning of their marriage, but now it was stronger than ever before. Just like metal that is hardened and strengthened by the heat of fire, their love for each other and Gott had been refined through trials and tribulations.

They'd proven that love was stronger than hate and that their faith in Gott was not misplaced. They'd weathered the storm and Holly was confident that no matter what the future held for them, they would handle it together. Gott was on their side and she could say with confidence that all was indeed well with the Miller familye. *Denke, Gott!*

* * * * *